MW00928613

The North Hollywood Detective Club

in

The Case of the

Deadly Double-Cross

Mike Mains

Published by Mystery Adventure Detective Books

"We read to know we are not alone."

Copyright © 2019 by Mike Mains

ISBN: 978-1-953006-00-4

All Rights Reserved. This is a work of fiction. Any resemblance to real people or incidents is purely coincidental. No part of this book may be reproduced or used in any form whatsoever or by any means, electronic or mechanical, or by any information storage and retrieval system, without written permission from the author. The exception being in cases of brief quotations embodied in critical articles or reviews. Cover by Pixel Perfect Publishing. Author contact: mainsmike@yahoo.com

Prologue

When the prison transport bus tipped and rolled over, Jeffrey Jones slammed against the wall amid a sea of shattered glass. Behind him, men screamed. Ahead of him, metal tore against metal, and the wire mesh wall that separated the prisoners from the driver and transport guard was ripped from its hinges.

The bus flipped twice and slammed to a stop. Jeffrey's head thumped against the wall and he fell to the floor, shards of broken glass in his hair. Above the pounding in his head he heard the moans of wounded men around him and the drumming of rain as it pelted the roof and beat against the windshield of the bus. He smelled oil and smoke and gasoline and the stench of burning rubber. The dim overhead lights sputtered and shut off, plunging the bus into darkness.

Jeffrey's glasses dangled from one ear. He raised a hand to straighten them, but his wrists were cuffed and attached to a belly chain around his waist and he could not reach them.

He leaned his head down and brought his legs, shackled at the ankles, up into a fetal position. Able to reach now, he adjusted his glasses. The first thing he saw was Pablo Reyes, shackled and cuffed, slipping through the mangled wire mesh wall and climbing over the crushed and lifeless body of the bus driver. Blood flowed from a gash on Pablo's forehead and smeared across his face. He gripped the steering wheel for leverage, swung his legs forward, and kicked out the remainder of the cracked windshield.

"Come on, Jeffrey," he said, and crawled out the windshield and onto the hood of the bus.

Jeffrey scuttled over the body of an unconscious prisoner and squeezed his frame through the twisted wire mesh wall. A prison transport guard lay dead on the floor behind the driver. Jeffrey reached inside the man's pocket and extracted a thick set of keys. Groans of injured prisoners filled the air behind him.

"Jeffrey, come on," Pablo called hoarsely from the hood of the bus. He saw Jeffrey fumbling with the keys and his eyes opened wide. "You got the keys!"

Jeffrey didn't respond. He worked feverishly, inserting one key after another into the lock on his handcuffs. Sweat speckled his forehead and dripped from his face onto his trembling hands. A police siren wailed in the distance. Jeffrey looked up and saw Pablo watching him through the broken windshield. Neither boy spoke.

Jeffrey tried another key, and another. A small L-shaped key slid in easily and popped the lock. He shook off the cuffs and tried more keys on the belly chain around his waist. Pablo watched tensely.

Jeffrey popped the lock on his belly chain and threw it away from his body. The first key he tried on his ankle cuffs unlocked them and he kicked them off. He scrambled over the dead body of the bus driver and crawled through the broken windshield. Pablo scooted aside and Jeffrey joined him in the rain on the hood of the bus. Broken glass from the windshield crinkled underneath them and pricked the skin of their knees and hands.

The overcast sky made the late afternoon seem like night. The wind drove the rain sideways. Pablo's face held an expression Jeffrey had never seen before: the desperate fear of an animal cornered.

Pablo brought his wrists forward and Jeffrey went to work with the keys. He unlocked Pablo's wrists, his belly chain, and his ankle cuffs, flung them aside, and turned back to the interior of the bus. A black prisoner, shackled and bloodied, crawled up the middle aisle. He looked up at Jeffrey with sorrowful, red-stained eyes. Jeffrey threw him the keys, and then he and Pablo slid off the hood of the bus and onto soft grass. Their orange prison jumpsuits were soaked and clung to their bodies.

They were at the foot of a small embankment, somewhere in East Los Angeles. Already a small crowd was gathering on the hill above, silhouettes against a gray sky. A police cruiser that had been accompanying the bus was smashed and sitting atop railroad tracks thirty yards away. Jeffrey and Pablo ran to it. Thunder boomed and a heavy torrent of rain poured down. The police siren continued to wail.

Jeffrey and Pablo stopped at the car and peered inside. The driver's side door was caved in, pinning a crumpled policeman behind the wheel. The man's left hand gripped the steering wheel, a wedding ring on the fourth finger. Jeffrey tried the door, but it was wedged in tight and impossible to open.

"Is he dead?" Pablo asked.

Jeffrey wasn't sure. His mind was spinning, dazed from the accident and the pelt of the rain. The policeman's bald head was ringed with blood. He looked dead. Laughter and shouts came from behind.

The boys turned to see six olive-skinned Hispanic men dressed in flannel shirts and khakis descending the small hill. Rain pelted their shaved heads and dripped from their chins and ears. They swept down the hill and headed towards the two boys.

One of the men, broad-faced and darker than the others, appeared to be their leader. A spider web tattoo began at the tip of his nose and spread across his face, covering everything but his cold black eyes. Jeffrey had never seen a more terrifying man.

The leader stepped past the boys and went directly to the police car. He lowered his head, cupped his hands to the side of his face and peered inside at the trapped driver.

Another man, thin and gangly, sidled up to Jeffrey and Pablo, looked them both up and down, and grinned through crooked teeth.

The leader turned away from the car and faced Jeffrey. "You're a cop killer, boy."

"We didn't kill him," Pablo said.

"Tell it to the judge," said one of the men, and the others laughed.

A groan came from the car. Jeffrey and the leader stared at each other for a moment, and then Jeffrey stepped past the man to the car and looked inside. The policeman behind the wheel rolled his head feebly and gazed up at Jeffrey with watery eyes.

"He's alive," Jeffrey shouted.

A train whistle shrieked.

All eyes turned to the sound. The blurry outline of a train appeared in the distance, approaching fast down the tracks.

"Not for long," said the man with crooked teeth.

Jeffrey turned to the leader. "We have to get this car off the tracks."

"For what, homie?" said the man with crooked teeth. "He was taking you to jail."

The police siren whined louder through the rain. The leader stepped close to Jeffrey, his flannel shirt buttoned up tight against a thick neck. He eyed Jeffrey's prison jumpsuit and said, "You better run, boy."

"We can't leave that policeman here to die," Jeffrey said.

The train whistle shrieked.

Jeffrey and Pablo broke for the car and scrambled around it, trying all the doors.

The men stepped closer. "You ain't getting him out of there," one of them said. "He's trapped behind that wheel."

The leader motioned sharply with his arm. "Get away from the car."

The men backed away.

"We have to get this car off the tracks before the train hits," Pablo said.

The leader stepped forward, grabbed Pablo by the front of his jumpsuit, and hurled him away from the car. Pablo stumbled across the grass. The leader barked an order in Spanish and two men grabbed Pablo, pinning his arms.

The leader turned to Jeffrey. "Did you hear me, boy?"

Jeffrey pointed to the car, his hand trembling. "If we don't get this car off the tracks, that man is going to die."

Anger flashed across the man's face. His fist was a blur in the rain. Jeffrey tried to duck and caught the blow behind his ear. It landed like a sledgehammer. He took a couple of crazy steps back and fell in the mud. Rain splattered the ground around him.

The man stood over Jeffrey and shouted, "He's a cop, let him die!"

Jeffrey scuttled backwards in the mud and rose shakily to his feet. "We can't do that."

The leader reached into the back pocket of his khaki pants and pulled out a switchblade knife. He eyed Jeffrey, nostrils flaring, and flicked the blade open.

Pablo shouted, "Run, Jeffrey!"

The man stepped closer through the rain, circling the knife in a smooth figure eight.

Jeffrey backed away, blood roaring in his ears. He saw the glistening blade of the knife and the fierce, tattooed face of the man holding it. He heard the train whistle screaming, the police siren wailing louder and louder, and Pablo's shouts.

What could he do?

What could he do?

Chapter One

"Stop that immediately."

"Stop what?"

"That infernal habit of yours."

Jeffrey blinked behind his glasses. "What infernal habit?"

Mr. Beasley, dressed impeccably in a three piece wool suit, rose up from behind his desk at the head of the classroom.

"Don't play dumb with me, Jones. You know precisely what I'm talking about."

Pencils stopped scribbling. Tenth grade students looked up from their test papers.

Mr. Beasley stepped out from behind his desk. "That infernal habit you have of gazing out the window and wishing you were someplace else. Let me remind you that at this very moment you are in my classroom, not lying on your backside in a field of clover, watching the clouds roll by; nor running barefoot on the farm, cavorting with the chickens and the cows."

The class chuckled and went back to their test papers.

Jeffery felt his face reddening and he squirmed in his seat. He was a stocky boy and the old wooden school desk groaned in protest under his weight. Like every male student in his school, he was dressed in a white short-sleeved shirt, dark pants and black shoes.

Marisol Rodriguez looked up from her test paper and her brown eyes opened wide. She wore the school uniform for girls: a white blouse and plaid skirt, black shoes and white socks. She brushed wavy strands of hair away from her face and turned to Jeffrey, seated across the aisle to her right.

Brian McHugh, seated in front of Jeffrey, spun around in his seat, a huge grin on his face. "Hey, barefoot boy, what are you doing with those chickens and cows?"

The class burst into laughter.

Pablo, seated behind Jeffrey, sat up straight and glared at Brian over Jeffrey's shoulder.

Brian noticed and said, "You got a problem, Reyes?"

"Yeah, you."

"That's enough," said Mr. Beasley, silencing the two boys.

Brian turned back in his seat and faced the front of the room.

Mr. Beasley cast his eye at Jeffrey. "As for you, barefoot boy ..."

Brian was the first to snicker.

"You have a test to take on the American Revolution. I suggest you get on with it."

"I'm done with the test," Jeffrey said.

"Impossible."

Jeffrey shrugged.

Mr. Beasley strode down the aisle and snatched Jeffrey's test paper off his desk. "Is this some kind of a joke?"

"It's not a joke. I finished it."

"And I say it's impossible. I designed this test myself. No human brain can complete it in less than fifty minutes."

"Jones isn't human," Brian said, "he's an alien."

The class laughed.

"Silence," said Mr. Beasley.

He marched back to the front of the room with Jeffrey's paper in hand and sat down behind his desk. He cleared his throat and studied Jeffrey's answers. After a few moments, he sighed and shook his head. "Jones, you never cease to amaze me. Every answer is correct."

Brian smirked. "Like I said, he's an alien."

Mr. Beasley looked at Brian and his eyes narrowed.

"I'll see your paper, as well."

"*My* paper?"

"That's what I said."

"Why do you want to see my paper?"

"Call it a hunch."

"But why?"

"Cease your stalling and bring me your paper immediately."

Brian turned in his seat and shot an angry look at Jeffrey.

"Don't look at him," said Mr. Beasley. "Bring me your paper."

Brian heaved his hulking body out of his seat and carried his test paper to the front of the classroom.

Mr. Beasley snatched the paper out of the boy's hand. "Take your seat."

Brian sulked his way back down the aisle, glowering at Jeffrey the whole way.

Jeffrey stared back, his eyes wide behind his glasses.

Marisol watched them both.

Mr. Beasley placed Brian's test paper on his desk next to Jeffrey's. Beginning with the first question, *Describe the state of the American colonies in the year 1776,* and ending with the last, *What was the true cause of the Revolutionary War?*, he compared their answers, tracing a line with his finger from one paper to the next. With each answer, his eyes clouded deeper with suspicion. When he reached the end, he grunted and said, "Just as I suspected, cheating."

The class gasped.

Brian spun around in his seat. "Did you copy my answers, Jones?"

Before Jeffrey could reply, Marisol said, "Jeffrey didn't copy anyone's answers."

Brian turned to her. "Who asked you?"

"Silence," said Mr. Beasley. He picked up both papers and held them aloft, one in each hand. "These test papers are identical, even down to the punctuation, and every answer is correct. That leaves only one logical conclusion: cheating." He slammed the papers down on his desk.

"Jeffrey doesn't cheat," Pablo said.

"Quiet," warned the teacher.

"But it's true," Marisol said. "Jeffrey doesn't cheat. Jeffrey would never cheat."

"If I want your opinion, Miss Rodriguez, I shall ask for it."

"Don't you know us by now, Mr. Beasley?" Pablo said. "I mean, after everything that happened last fall with the treasure hunt and the police and everything?"

"Of course, I know you. That's what makes this situation so perplexing." He paused and said. "Jones, I'm aware of both your intellect and your honesty, however, I still have my duty as a teacher and I cannot ignore the evidence here in front of me."

Jeffrey raised his hand. "Can I examine those papers?"

Brian leapt out of his seat, his ears red and flaring out from the side of his head. "What do you want to look at my paper for?" He turned to Mr. Beasley. "If anyone cheated, it's Jones. He was leaning over my shoulder while I was writing my answers. I could feel him breathing down my neck."

"That's not true," Jeffrey said, his voice rising.

"It is true," Brian said. "I swear to God."

"You lie!" Marisol said.

Brian swung around to face her. "I told you to stay out of this."

Pablo stood up and faced Brian. "Don't yell at her."

Brian turned to Pablo with clenched fists. "You want to fight about it, Reyes?"

Marisol watched with alarm. They were both six feet tall - the two tallest boys in their grade - but Brian outweighed Pablo by twenty pounds. His bulk filled the aisle.

Mr. Beasley rose to his feet and his voice boomed across the room. "Enough."

The two boys stood staring at each other.

"Sit down, both of you," Mr. Beasley said.

Neither boy moved.

"Now," said the teacher.

The boys broke off eye contact and slid into their seats.

"The rest of you go back to your tests."

Heads lowered and pencils resumed writing.

Mr. Beasley sat behind his desk. He looked at Brian and then at Jeffrey. "Jones, we'll start with you. I designed a very precise and detailed test on the American war for independence. I want to know how you managed to come up with all the right answers."

"The answers are in the book."

Mr. Beasley scowled. "I know the answers are in the book. What I want to know is how you managed to memorize such a wealth of information."

"I made a game out of it."

"A game?" said Mr. Beasley. "What do you mean a game?"

"I mean a memory trick."

"A *trick*?"

"I mean a way to remember. That's all."

"A memory trick to help you remember, eh?"

Jeffrey nodded. "I do it for all my tests."

Mr. Beasley frowned and leaned back in his chair. "Very well, let's hear it."

"Hear what?"

"This infernal memory trick of yours. If it's so helpful to you in passing tests, then perhaps it could benefit the entire class."

Heads looked up across the room.

Jeffrey stammered. "I don't understand."

Mr. Beasley leaned forward and stamped his desk with his index finger. "I want you to tell us this game, this memory trick you used that enabled you to pass my test in record time."

Jeffrey felt his face flush red. "Here?"

"No, in the parking lot outside. Yes, here. Do you take me for a fool?"

"No, sir."

"Then let's hear this trick of yours at once, and stand up when you address me."

"But, Mr. Beasley—"

"On your feet!"

Jeffrey stood up, his legs shaky.

School desks creaked around the room as students turned in their seats to stare at him. Mr. Beasley motioned at Jeffrey with his hand. "Begin."

The room fell silent. Jeffrey stared back at the gawking faces of his classmates. In that moment, he hated them all. All except Pablo and Marisol.

He began quietly, "In seventeen hundred and seventy-six—"

"Louder," said Mr. Beasley.

Jeffrey raised his voice. "In seventeen hundred and seventy-six, the thirteen colonies were in quite a fix. King George's boys were cracking down, on every village, hamlet, and town."

Mr. Beasley raised an eyebrow.

Jeffrey continued, "Nathan Hale was hung from gallows on high, for being a patriot and American spy. 'I regret that I have but one life,' he said, 'to give to my country,' and then he was dead."

Laughter rippled across the room.

A bead of perspiration popped at the root of Jeffrey's hair and ran cold down his forehead. He looked at Mr. Beasley, his eyes pleading for mercy.

"Go on," said the teacher.

"The Colonials countered on Christmas night, when George Washington crossed the Delaware in might. He caught the British by complete surprise, with a daring attack before sunrise. For that, old George won the victor's wreath. Not bad for a guy with wooden teeth."

The class howled with laughter.

Jeffrey felt a sudden weakness in his legs. He gripped his desk for support. "Benedict Arnold, not a traitor yet, forced a British retreat at Ridgefield, Connecticut. The Battle of Brandywine in seventy-seven, sent many to hell and few to Heaven. To turn the tide of battle now, an alliance with France was needed, but how? To convince the French to join the fight came old Ben Franklin, the man with the kite. Franklin sailed to France in seventy-eight. I wonder how many French fries he ate."

The class exploded in laughter.

Jeffrey felt the blood drain from his face. For a moment he thought he might faint. He grimaced, closed his eyes, and shouted over the shrieking laughter of his classmates. "The true cause of the war wasn't taxes or tea, it was gun confiscation by the British, you see. When those slimy Redcoats came for the guns, we rose up together and kicked their royal buns."

The class roared with laughter. Kids rolled back in their seats, stamped the floor with their feet and beat their desks with open hands. Brian doubled over with laughter, gripped his side and cried, "Jones, you're killing me!"

Even Pablo and Marisol joined in, unable to help themselves. Pablo threw his head back and laughed uproariously. Marisol laughed so hard she had tears in her eyes.

Mr. Beasley heard a faint humming sound and felt a buzz in his breast pocket. He reached in his pocket for his phone and glanced quickly at the text message he was sent: *Bring Jeffrey Jones to my office, please.*

Mr. Beasley pocketed the phone. "That's enough."

Jeffrey slid back into his seat, his face glistening and his shirt soaked with sweat. He took off his glasses and mopped his face with his sleeve.

Pablo gave Jeffrey a slap on the shoulder. "Good job."

Marisol wiped her eyes. "Jeffrey, that was great."

Jeffrey turned away, unable to face her. Marisol was the one person he most hated to be embarrassed in front of.

"I didn't tell you to sit down," said Mr. Beasley.

Jeffrey slid his glasses back on and scrambled to his feet.

Mr. Beasley stood up and crooked his finger. "Come with me." He pointed to Brian and Pablo. "And you, and you." To Pablo, he added, "And bring me your paper." He snatched Jeffrey and Brian's test papers off his desk.

Brian sat up straight, all merriment now gone from his face. "Where are we going?"

"You'll find out."

Mr. Beasley pointed to Marisol. "Miss Rodriguez, take charge of the class. Collect the test papers at the end of the hour." He stepped to the classroom door and swung it open, waiting. Jeffrey shuffled slowly to the front of the class, followed by Pablo and Brian. The three boys stepped into the hallway. Mr. Beasley stepped out behind them and closed the door.

"Where are we going?" Brian asked again.

"Follow me and keep your mouth closed." Mr. Beasley reached for Pablo's test paper, took it, and strode down the hallway. The boys followed, their shoes squeaking in unison on the tile floor.

Brian whispered, "This is your fault, Jones."

"Nothing's my fault," Jeffrey whispered back, "because I didn't do anything."

"Quiet in the ranks," said Mr. Beasley.

He led them past a long line of classrooms. At the end of the hall, an older male student acting as hall monitor stood waiting with a smirk on his face. Mr. Beasley and the boys strode past him.

The hall monitor looked them over, rocked back on his heels, and cackled under his breath. Pablo clenched his fist and spun around to face the boy, but Jeffrey grabbed his arm and steadied him. They continued walking.

Mr. Beasley opened the door to the administrative offices and waved the boys inside. Women staff members looked up from their desks. The teacher led the boys down another hall to an office with a sign on the door that read *Charles Popper, Principal*. He pointed to a bench outside the door. "Wait here."

The three boys sat on the hard wooden bench, Jeffrey in the middle. The teacher gave them all a long look, then opened the door to Mr. Popper's office and stepped inside. The door closed behind him.

Brian turned to Jeffrey. "Jones, I'm gonna kill you for this."

"You're not killing anyone," Pablo said.

"You stay out of this, Reyes. He's the one who copied my answers."

"Jeffrey didn't copy your answers. You copied his answers, we all know it."

"How can I copy his answers when he's sitting behind me?" Brian looked at Jeffrey. "Jones, did you see me turn around and look at your paper?"

"No."

"You see?"

"Then how did you get all the answers right?" Pablo asked.

"You think I'm dumb or something?"

"Well, you're not exactly the sharpest knife in the drawer."

Brian's ears flared out. He shoved Jeffrey hard into Pablo and both boys fell off the end of the bench and onto the floor.

Pablo grabbed the bench and heaved it up and forward, pitching Brian to the floor. In an instant, all three boys were on their feet, Pablo and Brian with their fists up, ready to throw punches, and Jeffrey standing between them, his arms outstretched to keep them apart. "Not in here," he whispered. "We'll all get expelled!"

Mr. Beasley's voice boomed from behind the door. "Enough!"

"Beasley's coming!" Jeffrey said.

The three boys leapt back to their positions on the bench.

The door to the principal's office opened and Mr. Beasley stepped out. Three innocent faces stared back at him.

"I heard a commotion."

"A commotion?" Pablo said, and glanced quickly at Jeffrey and Brian.

"What kind of a commotion?" Brian said.

"There's no commotion," Jeffrey said. "We're just sitting here, like three little mice."

Mr. Beasley raised an eyebrow. "Three little mice, is it?"

Pablo nodded. "Do you have a piece of cheese?"

"Yes, green and moldy." Mr. Beasley swung the door to the principal's office open wide and nodded his head sideways. "Inside."

The three boys rose, ashen-faced, and filed into the office.

Jeffrey had never been in Mr. Popper's office before and his eyes took in everything, beginning with Mr. Popper himself, sitting quietly behind a large desk. His elbows rested on the desktop, his slender fingers pressed together and the tips of his index fingers pressed against his lips. His skin was pale and looked as if it hadn't been exposed to the sun in years.

There was a cold efficiency about the man, and his office reflected it. The walls were bare and his desk was clear and spotless, save for a phone, a computer and the test papers of the three boys placed neatly before him. The boys lined up in front of his desk. Mr. Beasley stood to the side.

Jeffrey braced, not knowing what to expect. He knew he hadn't done anything wrong, but his mind began to swirl with visions of being suspended, of being expelled, of phone calls from the school principal to his parents, and then he suddenly imagined Mr. Charles Popper as the king of France, and Mr. Beasley as the king's executioner. All Beasley needed was a black hood over his head and a long-handled axe. Jeffrey wouldn't have to worry about anyone calling his parents. With a sneer of arrogance on his lips, King Charles would issue the command and then watch with delight as Jeffrey laid his neck down sideways on the desk, and Beasley wielded his executioner's axe and chopped off Jeffrey's head.

It was Brian's voice that snapped him back to reality.

"I'm telling you, I didn't do it. And if I did do it, it was an accident."

"Didn't do what, Brian?" said Mr. Popper.

"Whatever it is you're accusing me of doing."

Pablo's jaw dropped open. He looked first at Brian and then at Mr. Popper.

Mr. Popper leaned back in his chair. "I understand you had a test on the American Revolution this morning, and that you and Jeffrey had identical answers on your test papers."

"That's because Jones copied my answers."

"No, he didn't," Pablo said.

"Yes, he did." Brian said. "I tried to cover my paper," he mimed covering a paper with his hand, "but Jones kept looking over my shoulder at my answers. I could feel his breath on the back of my neck."

"That's a lie," Pablo said.

Brian pointed a finger at Pablo. "Sir, he's calling me a liar. He needs to be suspended."

"You need to be suspended," Pablo said.

"How about we suspend all three of you," said Mr. Beasley.

Pablo and Brian responded with an uproar of protest.

Jeffrey stood silently.

Mr. Popper waited until the two boys quieted and then said to Jeffrey, "How did you manage to get a perfect score on this test?"

Jeffrey glanced at Mr. Beasley. The teacher gave him a curt nod. "I used a memory game," Jeffrey said.

"A memory game?" Mr. Popper perked up. "I think I'd like to hear that."

Jeffrey glanced at Mr. Beasley with pleading eyes. The teacher caught his look and said to Mr. Popper, "Trust me, you don't."

Mr. Popper spoke to Jeffrey, "Did you copy Brian's answers?"

"No."

"He's lying," said Brian.

"You're lying," said Pablo.

Brian pointed a shaky hand at Pablo and shouted, "Sir, he needs to be suspended right now."

Pablo pointed back at Brian. "He's the one who needs to be suspended. He's been lying this whole time."

"Silence!" Mr. Beasley's command quieted the two boys. He gave them all a simmering look. "Three little mice, eh?"

"Three little mice?" said Mr. Popper.

"I'll explain later."

Mr. Popper surveyed the three boys standing before him. "Actually, my original concern wasn't with your test papers."

"It wasn't?" Brian said.

"No. I asked Mr. Beasley to bring Jeffrey to my office on a personal matter. He brought you and Pablo along so the two of you wouldn't fight while he was gone."

"Can I go then?" Brian turned to the door.

"Stand where you are," snapped Mr. Beasley.

Brian froze.

"This isn't the first time that your name has crossed my desk, Brian," said Mr. Popper. "You'll be sixteen this spring, am I right?"

"Yes, sir."

"How old are you, Pablo, fifteen?"

Pablo nodded. "I'll be sixteen in March."

"And you, Jeffrey?"

"I'll be sixteen soon, too."

"Then the three of you aren't boys anymore. You're men, young men. It's about time you began acting like it, which means this childish fighting of yours has got to stop."

"Reyes started it," said Brian.

"You started it," said Pablo.

"Enough," said Mr. Beasley.

Jeffrey held up his hand. "Mr. Popper, you said you wanted to see me on a personal matter?"

"Yes, it seems we had a little trouble here early this morning. Someone broke into the kitchen, stole some ice cream pies from one of our freezers. It's not that big of a deal really. But I thought it wouldn't hurt to have you give the scene a quick look and tell us what you think. I know you're pretty sharp when it comes to solving puzzles and crimes."

"When did the break-in occur?" Jeffrey asked.

"Around four o'clock this morning. No suspects, no arrests." He waved his arm dismissively. "But that's irrelevant now. What bothers me are these test papers. I've been a principal at this school for seven years. Before that I taught history for eight years. I know what students are capable of and I think I know cheating when I see it."

"As do I," said Mr. Beasley.

Mr. Popper looked at the three papers on his desk. "Pablo, your paper isn't complete, but it looks like most of your answers are correct."

"He's a cheater too," Brian said.

"Silence," said Mr. Beasley.

Pablo ignored Brian's remark. "I studied for over an hour last night, Mr. Popper," he said. "I went over every chapter in the book."

Mr. Popper nodded and looked up at Mr. Beasley.

"Guilt by association," the teacher said.

"What does that mean?" Pablo asked.

"It means that if your friend here is guilty of cheating," he nodded at Jeffrey, "then you likely are too."

"That's crazy."

"That's life."

Mr. Popper looked back down at Pablo's paper. After a long moment, he looked up and said, "I think we should flunk and suspend all three of you."

Pablo and Brian howled with protest, shouting and gesturing wildly with their arms. Mr. Popper regarded them each for a moment and then focused his eyes on Jeffrey. Jeffrey returned the principal's look without a flinch. When Pablo and Brian quieted, Mr. Popper said, "What do you say, Jeffrey?"

"I didn't cheat on the test. And I know Pablo didn't cheat. And Brian ... he probably didn't cheat either."

Brian shot Jeffrey a quick, surprised look.

"Then how do you explain the similarities between your and Brian's answers?" asked Mr. Popper.

Jeffrey shook his head. "I can't explain it."

"I can explain it," Brian said. "Jones copied my answers. He needs to be suspended. Both of these guys." He pointed at Jeffrey and Pablo.

Pablo started to speak, thought better of it and stopped.

Mr. Popper sighed and said, "I'll tell you what. I'll make you all a deal." The boys eyed him expectantly. "Jeffrey, I want you to take a look at the burglary we had in the kitchen this morning. The police don't know who did it. They said it was either a transient or a local gang member. If you can solve the crime and tell us who broke in, or at least provide a more satisfactory answer than the police did, we'll let this whole matter drop. You'll all receive a passing grade on the test."

Brian raised his hand. "What if Jones can't solve the crime?"

Mr. Popper leaned back in his chair. "Then all three of you flunk the test and all three of you are suspended."

Chapter Two

Yellow tape, emblazoned in black lettering with the words POLICE LINE DO NOT CROSS, stretched across the rear of the school kitchen. Bill Keller, the school janitor, mopped the floor just outside the tape. He wore a large set of keys on a metal ring clipped to his belt and with each movement of his mop the keys jangled.

Across the kitchen, water splashed in the sinks, knives chopped vegetables on cutting boards, and half-a-dozen female workers bustled about, chattering loudly in Spanish as they prepared the day's lunch menu.

A stout woman with short, orange-dyed hair strode up and down the aisles, overseeing the work. She had a pin in her nose and another pin in her eyebrow. The other women quieted as she neared them and resumed chattering after she passed.

A side door leading to the cafeteria opened and Jeffrey stepped into the kitchen. The first thing that hit him was the smell of meat loaf cooking in the ovens. He was in his second year of high school and meat loaf on Mondays remained his favorite item on the lunch menu. Meat loaf and green beans and mashed potatoes with gravy. He inhaled deeply. He could almost taste the food.

The stout woman saw him and shouted in a raspy voice, "Get out of the kitchen."

Keller and the kitchen workers looked up with surprise. Jeffrey stared back at the woman.

The woman reached for a carving knife. Her arms were big and round, and when she shook the knife, the flab on the back of her arm wobbled. "Did you hear me? I said out!"

Mr. Popper entered the kitchen behind Jeffrey, followed by Mr. Beasley, Pablo, and Brian. The woman pointed at the boys with her knife and spoke to Mr. Popper, "What are them boys doing in my kitchen?"

Mr. Popper approached her. "Gladys, I'm afraid you and your crew will have to excuse us for a few minutes."

"Excuse you for what?"

"We want to take a look at the break-in."

Gladys stabbed the knife down with a chunk into a wooden carving platter. "Students aren't allowed in the kitchen, Mr. Popper. You made that rule yourself. And besides, we need to get ready for lunch."

"You'll have time for that. Please." Mr. Popper spoke to the women workers in Spanish and motioned to the nearest door. Then he turned to Mr. Beasley and the three boys and motioned for them to step forward.

The women workers ambled out of the kitchen, casting curious looks back over their shoulders at the visitors.

"I don't like them boys," Gladys said in her husky voice. She nodded at Brian. "That big lug, he's here every day with a sob story about not having any lunch money. I know it's a lie, because his father's a rich hotshot, owns a swimming pool company."

"I'll talk to Brian," Mr. Popper said.

Gladys shook her head. "Won't do you any good." She nodded at Pablo. "That good-looking one, he shows up in line with his tray and my lunch ladies like to swoon all over themselves. When I'm not looking, they slip him extra cinnamon rolls. I ain't seen it, but I know they're doing it."

"I'll talk to Pablo."

Gladys shook her head. "Won't do you any good. But the worst one of the bunch, the one I can't stomach the most," she nodded at Jeffrey, "is that chunky one. Twice a day he's here, breakfast and lunch, and no matter what I serve, he eats it up."

Mr. Popper turned to her. "Isn't that the idea?"

Gladys threw up her hands. "How am I supposed to keep food in stock if he eats it all up?"

"Please, Gladys, just give us five minutes."

Gladys shook her head and followed the others out.

Keller stepped forward, mop in hand, keys jangling.

"I was fixing to clean the area, Mr. Popper."

"That's fine, Bill. I want Jeffrey to take a quick look first."

"Jeffrey?"

Mr. Popper nodded in Jeffrey's direction. "He's our resident Sherlock Holmes. If there's anything the police overlooked this morning, Jeffrey will find it."

"Is that a fact?" Keller's long bony face was suddenly very interested. He propped his mop up against the floor, wedged his armpit into the end of the mop handle and leaned into it to watch.

Jeffrey reached for the yellow police tape, stopped, and looked back at Mr. Popper.

"Go ahead," said Mr. Popper. "I doubt the police will be back."

"I'll need Pablo to help," Jeffrey said. "He's my partner."

Mr. Popper nodded his approval. Jeffrey lifted the yellow tape and squeezed his body under it. Pablo stepped over the tape. Brian started to follow them, but Mr. Beasley grabbed his arm and pulled him back.

Mr. Popper called to Jeffrey. "That freezer to your right is where the ice cream was stolen. There was an ice cream sandwich wrapper on the floor just in front of it. I guess the police took it."

"They didn't take it," said Keller, still leaning on his mop. "I threw it away."

Jeffrey stepped closer to the freezer and observed a broken padlock hanging from a clasp. "Is this freezer door kept locked?"

"Yes," said Mr. Popper. "The thief broke it. We have him on camera actually, but we can't see his face. He was wearing a hood and the image was very dark. He used the fire extinguisher on the wall to your left to smash open the padlock."

Jeffrey and Pablo turned to their left and stepped closer to the fire extinguisher. "What else did the camera show?" Jeffrey said.

"The parking lot camera shows him approaching from the field out back. He crossed the lot, came straight to the back door and kicked it open. Then he entered, used that fire extinguisher to break into the freezer, and stole an armload of ice cream pies. He ate one of them fast, threw the wrapper down on the floor, and went out the same way he came in, through the back door."

"Did the alarm go off?" Jeffrey asked.

"It went off the moment he kicked in the door."

"And then what happened, right after the alarm went off?"

Mr. Beasley spoke up, "I'm first on the contact list. I received a call from the alarm company, at precisely four o'clock this morning. They asked me if we wanted them to dispatch the police and I told them yes."

"There was a patrol car in the area," Mr. Popper said. "They arrived here at five minutes after four."

"I arrived at four-thirty," Mr. Beasley said. "The police were already here. I encountered the same scene you're seeing now. No suspect."

"Who sets the alarm at night?" Jeffrey asked.

Keller raised his hand. "That would be me, young man."

"What time did you set the alarm?" Jeffrey asked.

Keller turned to Mr. Popper. He wasn't accustomed to being questioned by tenth grade students. The principal gave him a nod.

"Five o'clock yesterday evening," Keller said. "That's when I finished cleaning. The alarm panel is by the gym door."

Mr. Popper said to Jeffrey, "Behind you is the door that the burglar kicked in."

Jeffrey and Pablo stepped to the back door. Pablo opened the door, it swung freely. "There's no damage," he said quietly.

Jeffrey turned to Mr. Popper and said, "There's no damage to the door."

Keller raised his hand. "I took care of that."

Pablo whispered to Jeffrey, "It's not easy to kick open a door, especially a thick one like this." He called to Mr. Popper. "How big was the guy who did this?"

"Pretty big. The way he picked up that fire extinguisher and slammed it down on the freezer padlock, he looked dangerous."

"Did he look like a gang member?" Pablo said.

"The image was hard to see, but he could have been. That's what the police said, either a gang member or a transient."

"This door is thick," Pablo said. "I don't think a transient could kick it open."

"Actually," said Mr. Beasley, "the policeman I spoke with had a theory about that. He told me the person in question was very likely high on phencyclidine."

"On what?" Pablo said.

Jeffrey answered, "It's a drug called angel dust."

"That's correct," Mr. Beasley said. "Some call it PCP. Others refer to it by its street name: angel dust. It's a mood altering drug. It can make a person think he has the strength to kick down a door and so he does. Mind over matter, you see. However, it comes with a cost. Those who imbibe it often end up in a coma."

Jeffrey reached for the light switch next to the door. He flipped the switch off, plunging the kitchen into darkness. After a moment he turned the lights back on.

"It's pretty dark in here without the lights," Jeffrey said. "Did the intruder have a flashlight?"

"No flashlight," Mr. Popper said. "The image on the camera was murky, like I said, but we could make it out."

Jeffrey stepped away from the door. Something caught his eye and he stopped to look at it. He pointed it out to Pablo: ragged gray flakes underneath a counter. Jeffrey lowered himself to his knees. He sniffed and peered under the counter and the nearby freezer.

Brian laughed and said, "This is retarded."

"Why is it retarded?" asked Mr. Popper.

"He's down there sniffing around like a dog."

Mr. Popper called, "What are you looking at, Jeffrey?"

"Ashes."

"Ashes?"

"Someone was smoking in here."

"Nobody smokes in the kitchen," Keller said.

Jeffrey stood up and looked at the janitor. "Somebody did."

"It couldn't be the person who broke in," Mr. Popper said. "We watched the whole video of him, he wasn't smoking."

"I thought you said you couldn't see his face, because he was wearing a hood."

Mr. Popper rocked back on his heels, his face reddened. "That's correct, but we didn't see any smoke coming from under his hood."

Pablo nudged Jeffrey and nodded at the countertop. Jeffrey looked and his eyes grew wide behind his glasses. On the countertop was the faint outline of a footprint.

"What size shoe do you wear?" Jeffrey asked Pablo.

"Ten."

Jeffrey tapped the countertop. Pablo hopped on top of the counter and placed his own footprint next to the first one.

"Now what?" said Mr. Popper.

"Footprint," Jeffrey said. "Somebody stood on this counter."

Pablo stepped back and Jeffrey examined both footprints. They looked identical in size. "Could be someone the same height as Pablo," he said.

Brian scoffed. "That's retarded. People of the same height have different shoe sizes." Mr. Popper turned to him. "Well, it's true," Brian said.

Jeffrey nodded. "Brian might be right. People of the same height do have different shoe sizes." He looked up at the ceiling panels. "Mr. Popper, what's above us here?"

"Teacher's lounge."

"What goes on up there?"

"Well, they lounge. Every teacher has a locker and their own chair. And they have refreshments."

"Is there a bar up there?" Brian said.

Mr. Popper answered him dismissively, "No, there's no bar."

Jeffrey thought for a moment. He asked, "Is there anything valuable in the teacher's lounge?"

"There's furniture," Mr. Popper said, "and a large screen television, computers, a vending machine, a copy machine ..." He turned to Mr. Beasley. "Am I leaving anything out?"

Mr. Beasley shook his head.

"Are students allowed in the teacher's lounge?" Jeffrey asked.

"Absolutely not," Mr. Beasley said. "In all my years in this school, not a single student has ever set foot in the teacher's lounge." He turned to Mr. Popper. "I'm rather proud of that. Why, it would be a scandal for a student to enter the teacher's lounge."

Jeffrey nodded to Pablo, still standing on the countertop. "Pablo, try those ceiling panels."

Pablo pushed up on the ceiling panel above him and moved it aside. He looked down and Jeffrey gave him a nod. Pablo reached high, gripped the open ends where he removed the ceiling panel, and hoisted himself up, disappearing into the ceiling.

The two men and Brian all stepped forward to watch.

Pablo called down, "I can crawl around up here."

"Can you get to the teacher's lounge from there?" Jeffrey said.

"I can try."

"Hold on," said Mr. Popper. "There are teachers in there right now taking their breaks. All we need is old Miss Hornsby seeing

Pablo's head poking up from the floor and she's liable to have a heart attack. Pablo, come down from there."

Pablo lowered himself down from the ceiling and back onto the countertop. He put the ceiling panel back in place and climbed down to the floor.

"Actually," Mr. Beasley said, "Pablo's head wouldn't poke up from the floor, but he could access the lounge through the vent. There's enough room in there for a person his size to fit through."

"So somebody could sneak into the teacher's lounge from here?" Jeffrey said.

The teacher nodded. "Theoretically, yes."

Mr. Popper shook his head. "This conversation is getting crazier by the second. Jeffrey, I already told you, we have the burglar on tape. We went over his every move. He kicked open the back door, broke into the freezer, and left. He never climbed onto that counter you're talking about."

"Are you absolutely positive?"

Mr. Popper hesitated. "Well, yes and no." He saw the confused look on Jeffrey's face and said, "Yes, I'm positive, because we have the intruder on camera the whole time he was in the kitchen and not once did he leave the frame. No, I'm not absolutely positive, because that counter you're standing next to is actually a blind spot."

"A blind spot? You mean from the camera?"

"Yes."

"So right now," Jeffrey said, "where I'm standing, the camera can't see me?"

"Correct."

"Are there cameras in the teacher's lounge?"

"No, we don't spy on our teachers."

"Only us kids, huh?" said Brian.

Mr. Popper blushed and said, "That's right."

"So somebody could go from here," Jeffrey rapped his knuckles on the countertop, "up through the ceiling," he pointed upward, "and then through the vent and into the teacher's lounge and the cameras wouldn't see him?"

"Correct, but it didn't happen so there's no point in discussing it."

"I think there is a point," Jeffrey said. Every eye turned his way. "I'm not saying you didn't see what you say you saw on the cameras, Mr. Popper, but I think there's more to this crime than meets the eye."

"Such as?"

"For one thing, like Pablo pointed out, that's a pretty thick door back there. It would be hard to kick open, especially for a transient who's malnourished and probably not in the best shape. So maybe the intruder was a gang member. Does it make sense for a gang member to go to all this trouble and risk going to jail just to steal a couple of ice cream pies? It's not logical."

Mr. Popper laughed. "You're talking about a crime, Jeffrey. Criminals aren't known for being pillars of logic."

"Criminals have logic," Jeffrey said. "It might not make sense to you or me, but it does to them."

"Unless they're on drugs," Pablo put in.

"Right, unless they're on drugs. If the intruder was high on angel dust, then my theory about the crime is wrong."

"Your theory?" Mr. Popper blinked. "And just what is your theory?"

"My theory," Jeffrey explained, "is based on logic. I say that somebody broke in just like you said, and stole some ice cream pies. But in addition to that, I say someone else, or possibly the same person, climbed up on this counter with the intent to break into the teacher's lounge above us or to go from there to another area of the school."

"I shall address your theory," Mr. Beasley said, "using your same sense of logic. In the first place, to access another area of the school from the teacher's lounge would require an intruder to exit the door that leads to senior hall. If he did that, then two additional alarms would go off, the first being connected to that door and the second being the motion detectors in the hallway. Neither of those alarms went off. Therefore, no such attempt was made. In the second place, nothing was stolen from the teacher's lounge. Computers, television, vending machine, everything is in tip-top shape. I was there this morning and saw for myself."

Jeffrey shrugged. "Maybe the burglar alarm scared them off. Maybe the thief didn't have time to steal what he wanted to steal."

Mr. Popper stepped forward. "Jeffrey, I can also dismiss your theory. And just like you, I can do it with logic. It makes absolutely no sense for a transient or a gang member to attempt to break into the teacher's lounge in the manner you're describing because," he paused for dramatic effect, "they would have no way of knowing it was even up there."

"That's the whole point," Jeffery said. "Whoever wanted to break into the teacher's lounge wasn't a transient or a gang member. It was someone who knew the teacher's lounge was above this kitchen and who also knew how to get up there. It's also someone who's been in this kitchen before."

Mr. Popper shook his head. "That's impossible."

"It's not impossible at all. You saw how dark it was in here with the lights out. Only a person who has been in this kitchen before would know there's a fire extinguisher on the wall. A transient or a gang member breaking in here for the first time wouldn't know that, and you said he didn't have a flashlight. Plus, there are ashes on the floor back here. That means the intruder was someone who felt comfortable enough being in the kitchen to take the time to smoke a cigarette. A typical burglar would never do that. They would be in a hurry to get in and out. Add it all up and it means only one thing: an inside job."

There was a moment of stunned silence before Mr. Popper burst into laughter. Brian and Keller joined him. Jeffrey, Pablo and Mr. Beasley watched the three of them with stoic faces.

Mr. Popper said, "Well this has certainly been entertaining. I've heard about your powers of deduction before, Jeffrey, but this is the first time I've actually had a chance to see your mind at work. I'll say this: you certainly have a vivid imagination."

"It's not my imagination."

Keller whistled low under his breath. When the others turned to him, he shook his head, picked up his mop and walked off.

"It's not my imagination," Jeffrey said again.

Mr. Popper sighed. "Jeffrey, I don't mean to hurt your feelings, but your theory doesn't hold water."

"My theory holds an ocean of water."

"But you can't answer the primary question of why somebody would want to break into the teacher's lounge to begin with."

"Then motive remains a mystery. But I stand by my theory."

"Me too," Pablo said.

Mr. Popper started to speak, but Brian cut him off: "I want to call my dad."

"About what?" said Mr. Popper.

"It's not fair, man. It's not fair for me to flunk my test and get suspended, because this idiot," Brian pointed at Jeffrey, "wants to play detective with some stupid theory about a burglar climbing through the ceiling into the teacher's lounge. For what? To steal a computer? To steal quarters from the candy machine?" Brian pointed at Mr. Beasley, "He said nothing was stolen from the teacher's lounge, isn't that right?"

Mr. Beasley nodded.

Brian turned back to Mr. Popper, "And you said you saw the guy on camera kick open the kitchen door and break into the freezer and never go anywhere else. Isn't that right?"

Mr. Popper nodded.

"All right then, case closed." Brian nodded at Jeffrey. "I know this guy. He thinks he's smarter than everyone else. He's talking about angel dust and burglars climbing through vents. If there's anyone high on angel dust, it's him. I'll tell you something else. I could feel his breath on the back on my neck while I was taking my test this morning. He leaned over my shoulder and copied all my answers. Whether you believe that or not, I don't care. You can believe what you want to believe, but I know it's true."

Brian continued. "So I want to call my dad. And I want to call a lawyer. I'm not going to flunk a test that I spent a lot of time studying for, because Jones here cheated and copied my answers. And I'm not going to get suspended either. It's not fair, Mr. Popper. It's not fair and you know it's not fair. You can't punish me like that just because Jones is delusional."

Mr. Popper heaved a heavy sigh. "Brian, you're right. You're absolutely right. You and Pablo can go back to class. I apologize to both of you. This was a mistake on my part. Believe me, it won't happen again. Mr. Beasley will escort you back to class." He looked at Mr. Beasley and the teacher nodded his approval.

Brian relaxed and stood waiting. Pablo frowned and shook his head. Jeffrey stood absolutely still, his face pale. Mr. Popper turned to him and said, "As for you, Jeffrey, we're going to have talk in my office."

Chapter Three

Jeffrey sat at a table across from Pablo and Marisol in the crowded school cafeteria and waved his empty fork in Pablo's direction. "So after you and Brian went back to class, Popper pulls me into his office and says, 'I just want to make sure I heard you correctly. You're saying the break-in was an inside job, somebody from this school?' I said, 'Yes, sir. That's exactly what I'm saying.' And he says, 'With all due respect, Jeffrey, I think you're wrong.' "

Jeffrey looked down at his lunch plate piled high with meatloaf, green beans and mashed potatoes and his eyes glistened. He speared a chunk of meat with his fork and popped it into his mouth. Pablo took a swig of milk from a half pint carton. Marisol glanced from one boy to the other and said, "Then what did you say, Jeffrey?"

"I said, 'With all due respect, Mr. Popper, I know I'm right.' "

Pablo laughed and choked on his milk. It spit out of his mouth in a long spray across the table.

Marisol shrieked and pushed her chair back from the table. Kids at surrounding tables laughed and pointed.

Pablo coughed and patted his upper chest. "I'm sorry." He grabbed a napkin off his lunch tray and wiped his face. "I'm sorry," he said again. "It's just when Jeffrey talks like that it cracks me up." He coughed some more and in his best imitation of Jeffrey's voice, he said, "With all due respect, sir, I know I'm right."

Jeffrey and Marisol both laughed, and Marisol scooted her chair back close to the table. Pablo grabbed another napkin from his tray and wiped milk off the table. "At least we both passed the test."

"So did I," said Marisol.

"So did Brian," said Jeffrey.

"You don't think he cheated?" Pablo asked.

"Of course he cheated," Jeffrey said. He lowered his voice and whispered, "He's the one who broke into the teacher's lounge." He popped a forkful of meatloaf in his mouth.

Pablo and Marisol turned to him with incredulous looks. "Are you serious?" Pablo said.

Jeffrey kept his mouth closed in a tight-lipped smile as he chewed. His two friends continued to stare at him with astonished looks on their faces, and he savored the feeling of keeping them in suspense. Finally, he swallowed and said, "I'm certain of it."

"But why?" Pablo said. "And how do you know that?"

"Let's start with some evidence. Exhibit A, the footprint on the countertop; it was the same size as your footprint, and you and Brian are the same height."

"Yeah, but that doesn't prove anything. Like Brian said, people of the same height can have different shoe sizes."

"I'll concede that point," Jeffrey said. "So Exhibit A is not conclusive. But what about Exhibit B? Beasley said no student had ever set foot in the teacher's lounge. Remember? He said he was proud of that."

"Right, I remember that."

"He also said they had a vending machine up there, but he didn't say what kind of vending machine. A little later, Brian said something about stealing quarters from a candy machine in the teacher's lounge. How does Brian know the vending machine in the teacher's lounge is a candy machine unless he's actually been up there himself?

Pablo snapped his fingers. "He did say that."

"Most vending machines are soda machines. There are also sandwich machines, coffee machines, potato chip machines. There are even machines to rent movies from, so how does Brian know it's a candy machine?"

"Brian could have heard someone say that," Marisol said. "He could have known it was a candy machine without seeing it himself."

"That's possible," Jeffrey said, "but not likely. Who would Brian have heard that from? He's not the type that talks to teachers. And how does he know the machine takes quarters unless he's actually seen it or put money in it himself? I've seen vending machines that only take dollars bills or credit cards."

Pablo nodded. "That's a good point too."

"Then there's Exhibit C," Jeffrey said. "Cui bono?"

"What's that mean?"

Marisol answered, "Who benefits?"

"Right," Jeffrey said. "Who besides Brian would have a reason to break into the teacher's lounge?"

Pablo shook his head. "I don't know. What reason would Brian have?"

"To steal the answers to Beasley's test."

"Whoa," said Pablo.

"Double whoa," said Marisol.

Jeffrey stabbed the table with his finger for emphasis. "Popper said every teacher has a locker up there. Those lockers probably don't even have locks on them, or if they do, the teachers keep them unlocked. So where's the most logical place for Beasley to keep his test answers? Beasley also said the teacher's lounge has a copy machine. So all Brian has to do is get the answers from Beasley's locker, make a copy, and then put the original back in Beasley's locker."

Pablo said, "That's how he got a perfect score on the test. Without those answers, he would have flunked."

Jeffrey gestured with his hands indicating agreement.

"Is Brian really that dumb?" Marisol asked.

"Trust me," Pablo said, "he's that dumb. If brains were chocolate, his wouldn't fill an M&M." He looked at Jeffrey. "I knew Brian cheated, but I didn't know how. The way you explained it makes perfect sense."

"It does make sense," Marisol said.

Pablo reached for his milk carton. "Jeffrey, you're the greatest, man." He lifted the carton in a toast and took a swig.

Marisol said to Jeffrey, "What are you going to do now?"

"Probably nothing. I don't want to get Brian in trouble, even though he's a jerk."

"He's more than a jerk," Pablo said. "He cheated on the test, but he accused you of cheating, and he tried to get us suspended."

Marisol raised her eyes in surprise. "Really?"

Pablo nodded. "He told Popper two or three times to suspend me and Jeffrey. The guy is scum."

Marisol looked at Jeffrey. "Are you sure you don't want to report him? If you did, he'd be expelled."

"Arrested too," Pablo said.

"Right." Jeffrey lowered his head, thought for a moment, and said, "It's not like he killed anyone. Nothing valuable was stolen, so the only person he hurt was himself. I won't rat him out."

"What about those ice cream sandwiches?" Pablo said. "And how did Brian kick in that back door? He's pretty strong, but not that strong. I'm as strong as he is and I don't think I could do it. Plus, Popper said the cameras show the person coming straight in and leaving."

"That's the tricky part." Jeffrey said. "We're actually dealing with two mysteries, both occurring around the same time. There's a connection between the two of them, I just don't know what it is."

"So are we on a new case?" Pablo said.

"We could be," Jeffrey answered, "there's just one thing—" His eyes focused on something directly behind Marisol and he stopped in mid-sentence.

Marisol turned and looked over her shoulder to see what Jeffrey was staring at. A smiling blond girl, dressed in the school uniform and striding with the confidence of an older student, approached their table. The girl stopped behind Marisol, green eyes gleaming, and said, "Are you Jeffrey?"

Jeffrey nodded. The girl said, "Hi, I'm Zinka." She smiled wide and extended her hand over the table. Jeffrey rose and bumped into the table. He started to extend his hand, stopped, wiped his palm on the side of his pants, and then reached again for Zinka's hand.

"I'm a senior," she said as they shook. "I'm new here. I heard about what you did this morning and I'm totally impressed."

"What did you hear?" Jeffrey said, his face reddening.

"About you solving the crime in the kitchen."

"Who told you about that?"

"Everyone's talking about it."

"Brian must have blabbed," Pablo said.

"I didn't solve anything," Jeffrey said.

"That's not what I heard."

Jeffrey tensed. In a guarded voice, he said, "What did you hear, exactly?"

"Just that you think it was an inside job, someone from this school. Do you have any idea who it might be?"

"Not really. I just came up with a working hypothesis."

"Well, it's an amazing hypothesis." She pointed to an empty chair at Jeffrey's side. "Can I sit down?"

"Sure." Jeffrey pulled the chair back for her. Zinka stepped around the table.

Pablo stood up, grabbed a napkin from his tray and wiped milk from the table in front of the empty seat. "Sorry," he said, "I choked on my milk." He dropped the napkin on the table and held out his hand. "Hi, I'm Pablo."

"Pablo! Yes! I heard about you too. You're like a team, right? You and Jeffrey?"

"Pretty much."

"That's awesome." She and Pablo shook hands and everyone sat down.

Marisol smiled and extended her hand across the table. "Hi, I'm Marisol."

Zinka ignored Marisol's hand and turned to Jeffrey. "I really need to ask you something."

Marisol withdrew her hand quickly and sat back. She glanced at the two boys, but neither seemed to notice. Their eyes were on the older blond girl.

"It's about my father," Zinka said.

"What about him?"

"Well, I've never met him. I'm adopted. My mother died at childbirth and my father gave me up for adoption." She glanced down at the table and then back up at Jeffrey. "I want you to find him."

Jeffrey studied the girl's somber face. "Aren't there ways of doing that?"

Zinka shook her head. "I've tried them." She made a flippant gesture with her hand. "Believe me, I've tried them all. I even hired a private detective, but everyone tells me the same thing. They all say it's impossible."

"Then how can we help you?"

"I think you're smart enough to do what other people can't."

Jeffrey laughed. "I wish my teachers all thought that."

"I'm sure they do, they just don't want you to know. Look, Jeffrey, I've heard a lot of good things about you. And you too, Pablo. Please, you've got to help me. You're my only hope."

"It's kind of hard to disappear," Jeffrey said. "The police or a private detective can track down just about anyone these days."

"Well they've all failed. So I'm thinking outside the box. I'm thinking maybe someone as smart as you might be able to do it."

Jeffrey shook his head. "It'll be like looking for a needle in a slaughterhouse. How do you even know what city he's in?"

"He's in Los Angeles."

"How do you know that?"

"The private detective I hired was able to trace him here. He also came up with this." She pulled a photograph from a pocket on her white blouse and handed it to Jeffrey. Pablo leaned over the table to look at it.

Jeffrey studied the photograph. It showed an ordinary-looking man from the chest up in front of a bookcase. The man looked to be about the same age as Jeffrey's father.

"How old is this picture?" Jeffrey asked.

"It was taken five years ago. His name's on the back."

Jeffrey flipped the photo over and read the words: *Ivan Dobic.* "So all you have is this picture and his name?" Jeffrey said. "Do you have anything else that might help to locate him?"

Zinka shook her head. "Unfortunately, no. Except that he was born and raised in London. I've never heard him speak, but he might have an English accent."

Pablo took a deep breath. "This *is* going to be like looking for a needle in a slaughterhouse."

"I'm sorry, Pablo," Zinka said. "I'm sorry, Jeffrey. I know it's not easy, but I think you can do it. And I'm willing to pay you." She pulled a small change purse from the pocket of her skirt and opened the little metal clasp. From the purse she extracted six crisp one hundred dollar bills and laid them on the table in front of Jeffrey.

Pablo stared at the money. Marisol stared at the girl.

"That's a lot of money," Jeffrey said.

"It's important to me that you find my father. Find him and I'll bonus you another six hundred." She pulled a pen from her pocket and reached for a napkin. "Here's my number and my email." She scribbled both on the napkin and handed it to Jeffrey. "My last name is Dobic, like my father. I trust you, Jeffrey." She gave his arm a quick squeeze. "Both of you." She reached across the table and gave Pablo's arm the same quick squeeze.

Marisol frowned, sat back in her chair, and folded her arms across her chest.

Zinka rose and the two boys did the same.

"We'll do whatever we can, Zinka." Pablo said.

"Thank you, Pablo. You're my only hope." She picked up the napkins Pablo used to wipe up his spilled milk. "I'll throw these away."

The boys watched Zinka walk off and then sat down. Pablo turned to the money on the table. "We're rich." He picked up one of the hundred dollar bills and held it up to the light.

"What are you doing?" Marisol asked him.

"Making sure these bills are real. The last thing we need is another case of counterfeit money."

Jeffrey started to laugh, but the serious look on Marisol's face stopped him. The bell rang.

"I gotta go," Pablo said. He handed the bill to Jeffrey. "Hold on to these, Jeffrey, until the case is over." He stood up, picked up his lunch tray and hurried off.

Marisol fidgeted in her seat.

"What's the matter?" Jeffrey said.

"I don't trust that girl."

"Why, because she didn't shake your hand?"

Marisol looked away in embarrassment. She didn't think either boy had noticed. "Not that."

"Then what?"

"She's a total stranger; why is she giving you all that money?"

"To find her father."

"Yeah, right."

"Some of this money is yours, you know." He pushed two of the bills across the table.

Marisol pushed the bills back. "I don't want it."

"You don't want to help?"

"Not this time. Not for her. That girl is a liar."

"How do you know?"

"I can tell."

"How?"

"Women's intuition."

Jeffrey laughed.

"It's not funny."

"I'm sorry. I'm not laughing at you."

"Yes, you are."

"We're investigators," Jeffrey said, "it's not necessary for us to like our clients. In fact, it might be better if we don't. That way our personal feelings won't cloud our judgment. We'll do what we always do, we'll proceed with logic and we'll play it safe."

"Look, I don't want to say you're in over your head, Jeffrey, because I know you're too smart for that. But I have a bad feeling about that girl. I think you should call it off."

"With all due respect, Marisol, I think you're wrong."

Marisol rose to her feet, pushed her chair in to the table, and said, "With all due respect, Jeffrey, I know I'm right."

Then she turned and walked away.

Chapter Four

"She wouldn't shake your hand?"

"Nope."

"That—"

"Don't say it." Marisol spun the combination on her locker and yanked the door open. Susie Norris stood at Marisol's side; her eyes wide behind her glasses.

"Well, she is," Susie said.

"I know, but I don't like that word." Marisol pulled a math book from her locker. "You should have seen Pablo. He was like, 'We'll do whatever we can, Zinka.' And she's like, 'Oh, thank you, Pablo, you're my only hope.' I wanted to throw up."

"Pablo said that? Does he like her?"

Marisol used her elbow to slam the locker door closed.

"He does, doesn't he?"

"He can like whoever he wants, I don't care."

"Yes, you do." The two girls turned and walked down the crowded high school hallway. Susie glanced at her friend as they wove their way through a stream of bustling students. "You know, you're feisty when you get jealous."

"I'm not jealous."

"Don't worry, I won't tell anyone."

"There's nothing to tell," Marisol said, her voice rising and drawing looks from other kids in the hallway.

"Shush," Susie said. "You're making a spectacle of yourself." The two girls turned a corner. "There's no need to be jealous. I mean, just because she's older than you, and blonder—"

"Will you stop?"

"I didn't say prettier," Susie said. "I know you're prettier than she is."

"Susie!"

Heads turned in the crowded hallway.

"I'm sorry. I won't say another word, not one more word."

Marisol stopped in front of a classroom door and Susie stopped next to her. "What are you doing?" Susie said.

Marisol cupped a hand to the side of her face and peered through the little window on the classroom door. The room was empty. She glanced both ways up and down the hall to see if anyone was watching and then quietly opened the door and slipped into the classroom.

"We're not supposed to go in there," Susie said. She looked quickly up and down the hall and whispered, "Did you hear me?"

Marisol reached through the open door, grabbed Susie by the arm, and pulled her into the classroom.

"Marisol!"

Marisol closed the door. "I want to show you something."

"But we're not supposed to be in here!"

Marisol stepped to the teacher's desk, opened the cover of her math book and pulled out a sheaf of folded papers. "If Jeffrey and Pablo can play detective, so can I."

Susie glanced nervously back at the door. "If someone catches us in here, we're dead meat."

Marisol unfolded the papers in her hand. "I have a copy of the student roster."

Susie gasped and stepped next to her. "Where did you get that?"

"Never mind where I got it."

"You stole it, didn't you?"

"I didn't *steal* it." Marisol spread the pages out on the teacher's desk. "I have friends in high places."

"Like who?"

"Like Chewy Garcia. He works Mondays after school in the administration office."

"Chewy Garcia has had a crush on you since the fifth grade."

"No, he hasn't."

"Yes, he has and you know it. That's why he stole it for you."

"He didn't steal it, he made me a copy."

"Same thing, you're not supposed to have it."

"Well, I do. And look," Marisol pointed to the pages. "This is a list of every student in our school, freshman to senior. There isn't a single person named Zinka on this entire list."

Susie scanned the list. "Maybe she goes by a different name."

"Then she lied to us when she told us her name was Zinka."

"Maybe Zinka is a nickname."

"Maybe, but she told us her last name is Dobic, and there isn't anyone with the last name of Dobic on this entire list either."

Susie looked up from the list of names and her eyes opened wide. "Then she *is* a liar. I hate her. I hate her and I don't even know her."

"I hate her too. I can't wait to see what Pablo says about this."

"I thought you didn't care about Pablo."

"I don't. My interest in this case is strictly professional."

"Uh-huh. Sure."

"I told Pablo we'd meet with him and Jeffrey tomorrow."

"Good luck getting Jeffrey to listen to you," Susie said.

Marisol folded the papers and slipped them back inside her math book. "Don't worry about Jeffrey," she said. "I know just how to talk to him."

"This is an interesting development," Jeffrey said.

He sat in his favorite bean bag chair in his bedroom in the basement of his house, and stared at the school roster list that Marisol had handed him.

Marisol and Susie sat across from him in a small two-seated sofa. Both girls leaned forward with expectant faces. They were dressed in their school uniforms and when Jeffrey looked up from the list of names his eye flashed to their bare knees. Marisol's knees were colored a golden brown; Susie's were white as snow. Pablo sat in a chair to the side.

"It's more than an interesting development," Marisol said. "It's proof that Zinka, or whatever her name is, lied to you."

"It's even more than that," Susie said. "It's proof that the great Jeffrey Jones has been conned."

"I haven't been conned by anyone," Jeffrey said.

Susie pointed to the list in his hand. "Looks like it to me."

"In the first place," Jeffrey said, "you weren't even there when we met this girl. In second place, what if she is lying? She paid us to find someone. She didn't ask us to do anything illegal."

Marisol's voice was urgent. "Don't you see, Jeffrey? This could be dangerous. If she's pretending to be a student and sneaking into our school, that's against the law. And how did she even know who you were? She singled you out in the middle of the cafeteria and walked right up to our table. She knows everything about you, and you don't know anything about her."

"Jeffrey's been conned," Susie said.

Jeffrey gave Susie a simmering look. "Is that the thanks I get for saving your hide?"

Susie blinked behind her glasses. "My what? Saving my what?"

"Your hide. For saving you from those crooked counterfeiters on our last case."

"I'm a human being, not a beast. I don't have a hide. I have skin, like all humans do."

"Fine, I saved your skin. Whatever."

"Whatever."

Jeffrey looked at Marisol and lifted the papers in his hand. "Where did you get this?" He saw Susie shoot a quick look at Marisol and he knew instantly that the two girls were hiding something.

"Never mind where I got it," Marisol said. "What's important is that Zinka's name isn't on it. She's not in last year's yearbook either, or the year before that. I checked them both. And how come none of us have ever seen her in school before?"

"She said she was new," Pablo said.

Jeffrey said, "That's probably why her name isn't on this list."

Marisol frowned. "Check the date, Jeffrey."

Jeffrey glanced at the list. "It's dated last Monday, the day we met her."

"Right, so that's a current list and her name's not on it." Marisol leaned back on the sofa. "People lie, Jeffrey."

"I know they do," Jeffrey snapped. His tone was dismissive and he regretted it immediately.

Marisol folded her arms across her chest and puffed out her lower lip. Pablo reached for the list and Jeffrey handed it to him.

"I'll tell you something else," Marisol said, "that blond hair of hers is fake. My cousin works in a beauty salon and she told me how to tell real hair from fake hair." Marisol lifted the black bangs that covered her forehead and pointed to the roots of her hair. "If you look close, you can see her roots are brown."

Jeffrey shrugged. "Okay, so her hair is fake. Don't a lot of girls dye their hair?"

"Some do, some don't. I never did."

"Me neither," said Susie.

"And what about her pretending to be a student at our school?" Marisol said. "Isn't that a crime?"

"I know it's a crime to impersonate a police officer," Jeffrey said, "but I don't know about impersonating a student."

"It's trespassing," Pablo said.

"So it is a crime," Susie said. "She sounds like a stalker."

Jeffrey scowled. "Why would anyone want to stalk me?"

"Because she's psycho," Susie said. "That hair dye of hers is seeping into her brain. It does that, you know."

Marisol said, "She's stalking you, Jeffrey, because she knows you're smart and she's using you to find this person, who probably isn't even her father."

Jeffrey looked Marisol straight in the eye. "I don't think the person she's trying to find is her father either."

Pablo sat up in surprise. "You don't?"

Before Jeffrey could answer, Susie clapped her hands and said, "You see! A stalker and a psycho."

Pablo held up his hand for quiet and said to Jeffrey. "Seriously, you don't think that's her dad in that picture she gave us?"

Jeffrey shook his head.

"Wow. Well if that's not her dad, then who is it?"

"That I don't know."

"I don't want any part of this," Marisol said.

"Me neither," Susie said. "What do you say, Pablo?"

Pablo shrugged. "I've heard both sides. Everyone makes a good point, but I think we're arguing for no reason. I mean, this whole thing is impossible to begin with. If the professionals couldn't find this guy, if a private detective couldn't find him, then what are the chances that we'll be able to? Plus, we don't even know if he's in Los Angeles. Zinka says he is, but we don't know that for sure. But let's say he is. There are ten million people living in Los Angeles county and four million people in the city itself. All we have to go by is a picture that's five years old. We might as well give Zinka her money back and tell her it's impossible. We're never going to find the guy."

The girls nodded in agreement.

Jeffrey said, "I've already found him."

Three astonished faces stared back at him.

"I used the picture she gave us," Jeffrey said. He reached to the nightstand next to his bed and picked up a manila folder. From inside the folder he pulled out the photo of Ivan Dobic.

Pablo pointed to the photo. "You used *that* picture to find a guy hidden in a city with millions of people?"

Jeffrey nodded. He held the photo for the others to see and pointed to the bookcase in the background. "The titles in these books are hard to see, but I used a magnifying glass and I was able to read them. They're chess books, so it seemed logical to me that the man in the photo was probably a chess player, and probably a pretty good one. So where do chess players go?"

"To chess clubs," Pablo said.

"Right, and how many chess clubs are there in this city?"

"There's one in Glendale," Pablo said, "and one in Santa Monica with these huge chess pieces, like three feet tall. They play on a giant chess board that's painted on the ground."

Jeffrey nodded. "The one that came to my mind is a park on La Cienega Boulevard where men go to play chess."

"I know that park," Pablo said. "I've driven by it with my dad."

"Me too," Jeffrey said. "So I went there yesterday after school. I called," he said to Pablo, "but you weren't home."

Pablo nodded. "My cousin was showing me how to ride his motorcycle."

Jeffrey continued, "So I went alone. It took me a long time to get there, but it was worth it, because I saw a guy playing chess who looked a lot like the man in this photo. He left on foot after an hour or so and I followed him to a house nearby. I kept trying to think of a way to figure out if he was born in London, like Zinka said. I thought of knocking on his door, but I didn't know what to say. Anyway, he came out after a few minutes to take his trash to the curb. So that was my chance."

"What did you do?" Susie asked.

"I noticed he was wearing a watch, so I changed my voice," Jeffrey switched to an English accent, "and I said 'Excuse me, sir.

Do you have the time?' He looked at me kind of surprised and said, 'Oh, from London, are you?' I said, 'How do you know?' He said, 'Your accent gives you away.' 'And you?' I said. 'London, born and raised,' he said." Jeffrey switched back to his normal voice. "Then he gave me the time and went back inside."

"So you think that's the guy Zinka's looking for?" Pablo said.

"I'm almost certain of it. However, there are a couple of things bothering me." Jeffrey tapped the photo. "These chess books in the background ... She told us this picture was five years old, but once I was able to read the titles on these books I checked the copyright dates on some of them and I found one that was published two years ago. So this picture can't possibly be five years old."

"Maybe she made a mistake," Pablo said. "She did say the picture came from the private detective she hired."

"That's possible, but there's a more likely explanation."

"What's that?"

"She lied. Something happened in the recent past that she didn't want us to know about or to investigate, so she told us this photo was five years old. Also, the man I saw looked exactly like this picture. He didn't look like he had aged five years. My guess is this picture was taken within the last twelve months."

"So what does all that mean?" Susie said.

Jeffrey looked at her. "It means were dealing with a mystery, and it means that Zinka," he looked at Marisol, "and I'm not so sure that's her real name either, is most likely a liar and not who she says she is."

"A liar is a liar is a liar," Pablo said.

"And she's a liar," Susie said.

Marisol leaned forward. "So you'll drop the case?"

"Well the case as far as we're concerned is solved. She hired us to find a man and we found him. We'll give Zinka the address of the man I saw playing chess, collect the rest of our money, and leave. After that it's out of our hands."

"Are you sure you want to do that?" Marisol asked.

"Why wouldn't we?" Pablo said.

"It could be a trap."

Pablo looked confused. "What kind of a trap?"

"Like I said before, she's using you. Both of you."

"Using us for what? We don't have any money. She's the one paying us."

"We'll go in the daytime on Saturday," Jeffrey said. "It should be safe then." He looked at Marisol. "You're welcome to join us."

"No way."

"Don't ask me to go either," Susie said.

"Don't worry," Jeffrey told her, "I wasn't planning on it."

"Good, cause I'm not going. I don't trust that girl at all."

Marisol said, "I know you, Jeffrey. You talk about logic and safety, but when you smell a mystery, you're off like a bloodhound. You get that look in your eye like a rooster before he attacks."

"Right," Susie nodded. "What she just said goes double for me."

"So if you were me," Jeffrey said, "what would you do?"

"I'd give her the money back," Marisol said, "and tell her you're not interested in the case."

"You'd give back six hundred dollars?"

Pablo raised his hand. "Plus a bonus, she said."

"Plus a bonus," Jeffrey said.

Pablo nodded. "I need that money to save up and buy a car."

"And where did Zinka get the money?" Marisol said.

Jeffrey shrugged. "Maybe she has a job. Not everyone is broke like we are." He turned to Susie. "As for you, you've never even met this girl. How can you judge someone you've never even met?"

"I don't have to meet her. I hate her without even seeing her."

Jeffrey threw up his hands.

"I told you he wouldn't listen," Susie said.

"I am listening," Jeffrey said, his voice rising.

"You see," Susie said, "now he's getting mad."

"I'm not mad, but I am getting irritated, because this whole conversation is ridiculous."

Marisol stood up. "Fine, Jeffrey. If that's what you think of me, I'll leave."

"No, I didn't mean you, Marisol. I mean this conversation, this idea that we're being set up in some kind of a trap."

"Which is the feeling I have about this whole case, which you think is ridiculous." Marisol's lower lip was quivering. "Pablo, can I talk to you? Alone?"

"Sure."

Jeffrey watched silently as Pablo and the two girls climbed the basement stairs, their shoes clunking up the wooden steps. He heard their footsteps scuff across the floor of the entrance hall upstairs, and then the sound of the front door as it opened and slammed closed. And then he was alone.

Outside, Susie waited on the sidewalk while Pablo and Marisol talked on the front porch.

"I mean it," Marisol said, "I've given both of you fair warning. Don't come looking to me for help if you end up in a trap."

"There you go with that trap again," Pablo said.

"Don't ask me to go for a ride with you in your car either."

"I don't have a car."

"You will with the money that girl is paying you."

"Oh, come on."

"I'm serious. Remember what happened on our last case with those counterfeiters? I tried to warn you, both of you, but you wouldn't listen. We all could've been killed."

"Yeah, but we stopped a crime."

"Yeah, but we all could've been killed."

"Yeah, but we stopped a crime. Look, we'll be okay. We'll go in the daytime on Saturday, like Jeffrey said."

Marisol made a futile gesture with her hands, turned, and walked towards Susie at the end of the driveway.

Pablo called after her. "We'll talk tomorrow."

Marisol ignored him.

Alone in his basement, Jeffrey sat and stared at the floor. He didn't mean to hurt Marisol's feelings, but he had. He thought his friends would be impressed by how quickly he'd found the man Zinka was searching for. Instead, he'd hurt the feelings of the one person in the world whose feelings he least wanted to hurt. How could he have been so stupid? He made a fist and punched it down hard on his thigh. *Stupid.* He wished he had never met the blond girl named Zinka.

Chapter Five

"Is this where she lives?" Pablo said.

Jeffrey checked the address on the slip of paper he held in his hand. "It's the address she gave me."

"How can she be going to our school if she lives out here?"

"Most likely she doesn't go to our school."

"So Marisol is right?"

The boys stood on the sidewalk of a residential street in an area of Los Angeles known as Koreatown, a good fifteen miles south of North Hollywood. Almost all of the houses and apartment buildings in the area were built decades ago, but each one had its own personality, its own charm. The two-story house in front of them was no different. It lay hidden behind a massive tree in the front lawn and a wall of bushes that needed a trim. Jeffrey saw that the lawn was neatly mowed, and that told him that the heavy growth of the bushes was not an accident; their purpose was likely to obscure the house from view. The question in his mind was why?

"Maybe she doesn't live here," Jeffrey said. "Maybe it's a relative's house." He looked up and down the quiet street. "It seems safe enough. Let's get our money and get out of here."

They crossed the front yard and rang the doorbell. A moment later, Zinka's head popped out from an open window on the second floor. "Jeffrey, hi! Come on in, the door's open."

The boys exchanged a look. Jeffrey reached for the doorknob and opened the door. He and Pablo stepped inside. The entrance hall was bare. So was a room to their right, which looked like a living room with white walls, beige carpeting and nothing else. When they closed the front door, all sound from outside ceased. It was eerily quiet.

"Come on up," Zinka called.

The stairs were covered in the same beige carpeting. Jeffrey and Pablo's shoes made no sound as they climbed the carpeted staircase and padded down the second floor hall. Jeffrey couldn't help thinking that the absence of sound from their footsteps and the whispered silence of the house made it the perfect location for a murder.

They found Zinka in a bedroom at the end of the hall on the second floor. The shades were drawn and the darkened room was filled with a dozen large cardboard boxes, most of them sealed with packing tape. Zinka stood among the boxes with a roll of tape in her hand. When she saw Jeffrey, she immediately broke into a smile, dropped the roll of tape, and stepped around the boxes. She threw her arms around his neck and hugged him.

Jeffrey felt the softness of the girl's body against his for a brief moment, and then she broke away, turned to Pablo and gave him a quick hug. She broke from Pablo and smiled shyly. "It's good to see you both."

She swept her arm over the roomful of boxes. "Sorry, I'm moving." She nodded to a light switch on the wall. "Jeffrey, can you get that light, it's getting a little dark in here." Jeffrey went to the light switch. Zinka motioned to Pablo. "Can you hand me that knife?" She pointed to a knife on top of one of the boxes.

Jeffrey flicked the switch on the wall. With the room bathed in light, he studied the girl before him. Dressed in jeans and a white button-down shirt, she looked different than when they saw her at school. She seemed older, more refined. He guessed her real age to be nineteen or twenty. His eyes went to her hair and he saw what Marisol had noticed: brown roots at the base of her hairline.

Pablo handed Zinka the knife. She took it gingerly by the blade and set it atop a box alongside the roll of packing tape. She wiped her hands on her jeans, and smiled. "So, your email said you had some good news for me."

Jeffrey nodded. "I think we found your father."

Zinka looked shocked. Jeffrey told her how he went to the park on La Cienega Boulevard and spotted a man who looked like the one in the photograph she gave them. "I followed him to this address," Jeffrey said, and handed her a slip of paper with the address written on it. "I don't know if he was born in London, but he spoke with an English accent."

Zinka stared at the slip of paper in her hand. She rubbed her finger across the outside of her left eye, as if to wipe away a tear, and then did the same with her right eye. "I'm sorry," she said, "I'm just ... it's my father." She sniffled and turned away.

Pablo turned to Jeffrey. Jeffrey kept his eyes on the girl.

After a moment, Zinka turned back to face them and forced a smile. "I promised you a bonus." She reached in her pocket for her little change purse, opened the metal clasp and pulled out six bills, all hundreds. She handed the bills to Jeffrey. The boys thanked her, but she waved away their appreciation and sat down on one of the boxes. She stared at the slip of paper with the address on it.

Jeffrey waited for Zinka to speak, but she said nothing. "So that's it?" he said. "We're good?"

"We're good," Zinka replied, without looking up.

"We'll see you in school," Pablo said.

Zinka did not respond. Pablo looked at Jeffrey and shrugged.

"We'll let ourselves out," Jeffrey said. The two boys left the room, walked down the carpeted stairs and left the house.

Outside, Pablo said, "That was weird, but at least we got paid."

Jeffrey said, "Did you see the way she wiped her eyes?"

"Yeah, it looked like she was crying."

"When a person cries, they cry out of both eyes and they wipe both eyes at the same time. She didn't do that. She wiped one eye and then the other, and afterwards her face was dry. There were no real tears."

"She faked it? Does that mean she's a psycho, like Susie said?"

"Maybe not a psycho, but she could be a psychopath." Jeffrey saw the confusion on Pablo's face and explained the difference. "People that are psycho are crazy. They hear voices and experience delusions. Psychopaths aren't like that. They're not insane, they just have no remorse so they can do horrible things to other people and not feel bad about it at all. Psychopaths are also compulsive liars and manipulators. They make great politicians."

Pablo shuddered. "I'm just glad this case is over."

The boys walked down the sidewalk. They did not see Zinka watching them from the second floor window of the house, nor the shadow of a man stepping up close behind her.

Chapter Six

Jeffrey sat in the passenger seat of his mother's car as she drove back from a trip to the supermarket. A heavy rain that morning had fallen off to a drizzle. The raindrops tapped a gentle patter on the car roof. The windshield wipers swept rhythmically back and forth with a soothing tick-swoosh.

Jeffrey stared out the window and mulled over the events of the last two weeks: He and Pablo had pocketed six hundred dollars each for a job that had taken very little of their time, Marisol was no longer mad, and Susie had stopped pestering him. Life was good. He turned to his mother.

"How much does insurance cost when you buy a car, Mom?"

His mother gripped the steering wheel tightly, her face etched taut in concentration. "Depends."

"On what?"

"On who's doing the buying."

"What about like me?"

"Shhh, Jeffrey. Please. Not now. I'm trying to concentrate."

"What's the matter?"

"You know I don't like driving in the rain."

"It's barely raining."

"It's raining enough." She turned the wheel. "Besides you're not sixteen yet."

"I'll be sixteen soon."

"We can talk about it then."

"Why can't we talk about it now?"

A car behind them blared its horn. Jeffrey turned around to look.

"He wants me to go faster," his mother said. "I'm driving slow."

She rolled her window down, stuck her arm out and waved for the car to pass. The car sped past them, horn blaring. Jeffrey's mother honked her own car horn back in response and shouted an insult that the driver of the passing car never heard.

Jeffrey frowned and shook his head.

His mother saw him and said, "Don't make that face at me. You know I don't like driving in the rain. It doesn't rain very often in this city, so oil builds up on the roads. Then when it does rain, the roads become slippery. I told you before."

Jeffrey ignored her and stared out the window. He knew he was being selfish, but a part of him didn't care. Soon he'd have his own car, and then he could drive himself wherever he wanted to go. Pablo too. They both had to start thinking about getting their driver's licenses and buying their first cars. To do that, they needed to save money. The cash that Zinka paid them was a start.

The rain seemed to be slowing down. Jeffrey's mother turned the car onto their street. Jeffrey noticed an unfamiliar black sedan parked in front of their house. He sat up straight. There was something amiss, something he didn't understand.

A white van rushed past them from behind. As soon as it passed, the driver cut into their lane and slammed the brakes.

Jeffrey's mother screamed and jammed her foot down on the brake pedal. Tires skid against wet pavement. Jeffrey lurched forward. His seatbelt strap bit into his shoulder and then snapped his body back. His mother's car slid to a stop. The van in front of them stopped also. The doors on the van popped open and four men wearing police jackets and holding guns jumped out.

An identical white van stopped behind their car, blocking any escape. More men came running from the second van. Jeffrey and his mother were surrounded by men with guns.

The men were all yelling at once, guns pointed, faces tense. Jeffrey's mother screamed. Jeffrey put his hands up. A policeman just outside his window pointed his gun directly at Jeffrey's head and screamed at him to keep his hands up and exit the vehicle.

"I'm wearing a seat belt," Jeffrey yelled back.

The policeman shifted his gun to one hand and used his other hand to pop open Jeffrey's door. Other men moved in to cover him. Four guns pointed at Jeffrey's head, another four pointed at his hysterical mother.

The policeman shouted at Jeffrey, "Keep your left hand up. Use your right hand and unfasten the seat belt."

Jeffrey unclipped the seat belt.

The policeman stepped back.

"Now get out of the car."

"Alright, alright, alright ... Don't shoot."

Jeffrey stepped gingerly out of the vehicle, his hands raised high. The men stepped back.

"Turn around, get on your knees."

Jeffrey followed instructions. Within seconds, he was searched for weapons and his hands were cuffed behind his back.

"Jeffrey Jones?" a voice said.

"Yes."

"You're under arrest – for murder."

Chapter Seven

The prosecutor for the state of California was an attractive woman of Jamaican and East Indian descent. She pointed a finger at Jeffrey and Pablo as they sat with their attorneys at the defense table and said to the jury, "The state will prove, beyond any shadow of a doubt, that the two defendants seated before you did willfully and maliciously commit an act of cold-blooded murder. The evidence will show that they acted alone in this crime. And the state will ask that you convict them both of first-degree murder and send them both to prison for the remainder of their lives."

The boys sat stoically, dressed in suits, and watched as the prosecutor laid out her case. The man that Zinka had hired them to find was found murdered in his West Los Angeles home. His real name was William Hodges and the police report indicated that he had been strapped to a chair and tortured for two hours with knife slashes and cuts before finally dying from a fatal stab wound to the heart.

Hodges' home had been ransacked, the drawers of his desk and dresser pulled out and their contents spilled onto the floor; the clothes in his closets pulled off their hangers and dumped on the floor; every drawer and cabinet in his kitchen opened and searched through. The consensus of the homicide detectives investigating the case was that the murderers were after money.

The police were led to Jeffrey and Pablo by an anonymous tipster that alerted them to the crime. They had Jeffrey on surveillance video from the park on La Cienega Boulevard. It showed him watching Hodges as he played chess, and then following Hodges as he left the park. They had Jeffrey's fingerprints on the front doorknob of the man's home, and on a light switch in the bedroom where Hodges was killed. They had Pablo's fingerprints on the murder weapon, a knife plunged deep into the victim's chest. They had Pablo's DNA under the dead man's fingernails.

After Jeffrey's arrest, they searched his bedroom and found the picture of Hodges that Zinka had given him. They also found the money each boy was carrying that Zinka had paid them. The serial numbers on the hundred dollar bills Jeffrey and Pablo had ran in consecutive order with a small stack of hundred dollar bills that the police found hidden under a chair in the victim's home, money that the police said was overlooked by the killers.

Because of the viciousness of the murder, the boys were being tried as adults, with the prosecutor seeking life imprisonment without the possibility of parole. If not for their age, she would have sought the death penalty.

To the policemen and homicide detectives involved, it was an easily solved case. To the prosecutor, it was an easy conviction. To Jeffrey, it was an easy frame.

When he first heard the details of the gruesome murder, Jeffrey immediately pieced together how he and Pablo were set up. He explained it all in his first meeting with his attorney. "Yes, I followed that man from the park on La Cienega, because I was paid to find him by that girl Zinka I told you about."

The attorney, a thin man in glasses, nodded.

"When I went with Pablo to see Zinka at a house in Koreatown, she called to us from an upstairs window and told me the front door was unlocked, so I opened it. I also closed the door once we were inside. That got my fingerprints on the doorknob. When we were on the second floor of the house, she told me to turn on a light. That got my fingerprints on the light switch. The doorknob and the light fixture were then switched with the ones at the house where the guy was murdered, probably right after he was killed. So now my fingerprints are at the murder scene."

"What about the murder weapon?" the attorney said.

"Zinka told Pablo to hand her a knife when we were inside the house. That got his fingerprints on a knife. Hodges was probably killed with an identical knife, but the one with Pablo's fingerprints on it was left at the scene."

"And Pablo's DNA? How did they get that under the fingernails of the victim?"

"Easy. Before Zinka came to our table in the school cafeteria, Pablo laughed and spit out some milk. He used some paper napkins to wipe it up. Zinka took those napkins with her when she left. They had Pablo's DNA from his saliva."

"So who killed William Hodges, this Zinka girl?"

"I don't know if she did the actual killing," Jeffrey said. "It was probably a male accomplice, maybe several male accomplices. But she's the one who framed me and Pablo. She's the one that got Pablo's DNA and both of our fingerprints and then planted them at the crime scene. She's the one who hired us to begin with."

"How do you explain the six hundred dollars in cash each of you boys were carrying? The serial numbers on those bills were consecutive to the serial numbers on bills found in the victim's home."

"Obviously, that was part of the frame. Somebody withdrew a few thousand dollars from the bank, all in hundreds. Then Zinka paid us each six hundred dollars and planted the rest of the money at the crime scene. Just one more thing to make us look guilty."

The attorney sat back in his chair. "The way you explain it, everything makes sense. But your whole case hinges on this mystery girl, this Zinka. Nobody else has seen her, only you, Pablo and your friend, Marisol Rodriguez. And that house in Koreatown where you met her, the owner says no one lives there and it's been vacant for over a year."

"Either the owner of the house is lying," Jeffrey said, "or Zinka knew it was vacant and used it to fool us. What about the surveillance video from the cameras in our school cafeteria? Don't they show her coming to our table at lunchtime and talking to us?"

"I looked into that. Apparently, the cameras were turned off that day."

Jeffrey slapped the table with the flat of his hand. "That doesn't make sense."

"Wait a second, actually it does. There was a burglary at your school earlier that morning. Your principal, name of Charles Popper, requested the video from the alarm company. Somehow in that transaction, the cameras for the whole school were turned off. They didn't get turned back on until late that afternoon. So it appears to be an honest mistake, unless you think this Popper character is somehow involved with the murder."

"No, not Mr. Popper." Jeffrey shook his head. "This whole case is stupid and retarded. I wouldn't know how to torture and murder someone even if I wanted to. That prosecutor has to know that."

"Of course, she knows it. But she has political ambitions. She wants to run for Attorney General in the state of California, and then for governor, and then maybe for president. There's nothing she'd like better than to send a white middle-class kid like you to prison for the rest of his life. In this state, it's almost guaranteed to get her elected."

Jeffrey's eyes opened wide. "That's not fair."

The attorney's face was taut. "Welcome to the real world."

From the day of his arrest, Jeffrey knew his survival depended on strength. He began doing pushups alone in his cell. At first he couldn't do one, so he lowered his body only halfway down. He did this several times a day and within a week he was able to complete a full repetition, lowering his body until his chest touched the floor and then pushing back up. Soon he was able to do five pushups, and he began doing a set of pushups every hour or two throughout the day.

Pablo had once told him it was good to exercise hard, but not to push to the point of exhaustion, so Jeffrey followed that advice, stopping his sets one or two reps short of his limit. He also varied the intensity, pushing harder and doing more sets and repetitions on some days than others. Within two weeks he was doing twenty-five pushups a day. In another two weeks he was up to fifty a day, and then seventy-five, never pushing to his absolute limit, but sometimes coming close. On those higher-intensity days, when he neared the end of a set and sweat was pouring off his brow and dripping to the floor, he thought of Marisol and he pushed out one or two more repetitions.

Why her? He didn't know. She was pretty; he'd noticed that the first time he saw her back in the second grade. But there had to be more. Was it the way she seemed to read his thoughts, to always know exactly what he was thinking? That must be it, he decided. But then, only moments later, he changed his mind. There had to be more to it than that.

Before his arrest, a time that now seemed like the distant past, he thought of her often. Sometimes at night – always at night – he would lie in bed and imagine what it would be like to marry her. It was a dream mixed with guilt, because he knew she liked Pablo and Pablo liked her. He also knew it was never going to happen. Still it made him feel better to imagine it. No matter how twisted his life was, he could always think of Marisol and feel better. It was a private secret he held. A secret he would take to the grave.

Marisol wasn't the only girl he thought of. He also thought of Susie. She wasn't bad-looking, he mused. Actually, she was kind of cute. Not like Marisol, but in her own way. Too bad her sarcasm ruined everything. If Susie could only keep her mouth shut, he thought, maybe he could find a way to like her too.

To Jeffrey's exercise routine, he added sit-ups for his stomach and deep knee bends for his lower body, squatting as far down as he could go and then pressing up with his thigh and glute muscles. Some days he skipped those exercises, but he always did his pushups. After every set of pushups, he flexed and tensed his muscles, holding the contractions for five or six seconds.

Together with the meager rations of jailhouse food he was given, his body began to take on a chiseled, muscular appearance.

His jaw looked harder and more defined. The transformation was startling.

Pablo noticed and whispered to him before the start of a court appearance, "You look strong, man. You look like a hulk." Pablo had been doing his own pushups and he looked stronger and more muscular than Jeffrey had ever seen him. Jeffrey whispered back, "You too."

Jeffrey and Pablo weren't the only ones whose appearance was changing. Each day the prosecutor wore shorter and shorter skirts to court and each week she strode into the courtroom with a new hairstyle. Jeffrey noticed that every time the prosecutor presented something dramatic in court she made it a point to position herself so she was facing a section of the courtroom where a group of reporters were gathered. The next day her picture would be featured dramatically on the front page of the local newspaper and on the home page of every major news site. It made Jeffrey sick to watch.

Marisol testified as a witness and told the court how she and the two boys were approached by Zinka in the school cafeteria. The prosecutor disputed Marisol's testimony and called her a liar.

Father Pat, a Catholic priest and an old friend of the two boys and their families, testified as a character witness. The prosecutor painted him as a senile old man.

Jeffrey and Pablo both testified and stuck vehemently to their stories. The prosecutor tore into their testimony with relish and called them liars and ruthless killers. The attorneys for the boys objected numerous times, but the judge, a woman in her sixties with a perpetual scowl, frizzy gray hair and lips painted pink, overruled them every time.

In a private meeting, Jeffrey's attorney explained the judge's behavior: "She's up for reelection." Jeffrey's stunned expression prompted the attorney to continue. "This is a high profile case, lots of media attention. If you're acquitted, everyone will forget about it and it won't do her any good. But if you're convicted, then she can sentence you to life in prison and that will go down strong with the voters. It's something they'll remember, something she can run her reelection campaign on."

"Doesn't anyone care about the truth?" Jeffrey said.

The attorney frowned. "It's hard to get someone to believe the truth when their position in life depends upon their believing a lie. You've got to understand something. Everyone involved in this case – the prosecution, the judge, the cops, everyone – has an agenda, and that agenda is how they can best use this case to further their professional position. Truth means nothing to these people. What they care about is winning.

"It's the same with those reporters you see in court every day. If you're acquitted, it's a nothing story and nobody cares. But if you're convicted, they can milk that story for days, weeks, months even. They're milking it right now. And the more eyes on a story, the more money they make from advertising. A guilty verdict in a high-profile homicide case like this is perfect for them. It's like throwing a juicy steak to a ravenous wolf.

"You're young," the attorney continued, "you don't understand how the world works." Jeffrey started to protest, but the attorney held up his hand. "I know, I know, you're a smart kid. Smarter than most adults, that's for sure. And you *think* you know how life works, but you really don't. You're missing the most important part of the equation."

"What's that?" Jeffrey asked.

"The world is run by evil people," the attorney said, "evil men and evil women. Most people don't want to hear that. They're either too stupid to comprehend it or they know it's true, but they choose to ignore it. Once you know the truth, childhood is over. Once you know the truth, you can never go back."

Jeffrey sat in stunned silence.

"I'm sorry to be the one to tell you," the attorney said, "but that's just the way it is."

Under cross examination, the prosecutor approached Jeffrey as he sat on the witness stand. "You claim that a doorknob with your fingerprints on it was switched with a doorknob at the scene of the crime."

Jeffrey nodded. "That's correct."

"And just when did this switch take place?"

"I don't know."

"Oh, you don't know?"

"I don't know the exact date or time. It was after Pablo and I left the house in Koreatown where we met with Zinka."

"Zinka, the girl you claim to have met at your school?"

"The girl I *did* meet at my school."

The prosecutor turned to the jury. "It may please the jury to know that while the defendant does not know when this alleged doorknob switch took place, the state of California does know." The prosecutor positioned herself in front of the pool of courtroom reporters. When she had their full and undivided attention, she said, "It occurred last night at midnight, in the defendant's dreams."

The court burst into laughter.

Jeffrey's eyes immediately went to the judge. He saw her cover a smile with her hand. Members of the jury did the same.

Jeffrey's lawyer leapt to his feet and shouted, "Objection."

The judge replied, "Overruled."

It took every ounce of self-control for Jeffrey not to stand up in court and tell both the prosecutor and the judge what he really thought of them.

Days passed. The trial went on. The strain on Jeffrey and Pablo's parents was enormous. Both families had cleaned out their bank accounts and mortgaged their homes to pay for defense lawyers. Each day they sat in court, ashen-faced, and watched the proceedings. Each day it seemed more and more as if the entire trial was a sham. Jeffrey felt worse for the pain his parents were going through than for his own.

Marisol attended court when she could, skipping school and sitting by herself in the middle of the gallery. School meant nothing to her now. If the boys were convicted then life itself was meaningless. Jeffrey and Pablo saw her and shot looks her way whenever they could. She occupied both of their minds.

Susie's parents forbade her to attend the proceedings. In their eyes, and in the eyes of almost everyone else in their community, the two boys were guilty.

Jeffrey began to pray like never before. Every morning and every night he poured his heart out to God and pleaded for help. He wasn't allowed to have a Rosary in his cell, so he used his fingers to count the decades. Prayer had never failed him in the past, so he trusted it would not fail him now. However, with each passing day, his doubts grew heavier. With each passing day, his situation appeared more hopeless.

And then the fateful day arrived when the jury reached their verdict. Pablo was hopeful, but Jeffrey studied the jurors as they filed back into the courtroom and took their seats. None of them looked his way. His heart sank immediately. He didn't tell Pablo what his mind already knew.

The verdict, written on a slip of paper, was handed to the bailiff, passed to the judge who read it for herself, and then passed to the court clerk. On the judge's order, the two boys rose and faced the jury. Their parents stiffened with fear. The courtroom was silent. The clerk unfolded the slip of paper and read aloud the verdict: Guilty.

The word hung like a death knell over the crowded courtroom. Reporters and spectators gasped. The mothers of both boys burst into tears. Their fathers sat stone-faced, devoid of color and stunned. The prosecutor smiled smugly and turned to face the reporters.

Marisol stood up from her seat in the middle of court and cried, "That's a lie! They're innocent!"

Her outburst brought more gasps, and every eye in the crowded courtroom turned her way. The angry judge banged her gavel. A huge bailiff appeared quickly, took Marisol by the arm and yanked her away from her seat. She continued to yell as the bailiff pulled her toward the door.

Half-a-dozen other bailiffs surrounded the two boys and hustled them past their attorneys and towards a side door. Jeffrey caught one last look at Marisol being dragged out of court, and then a hurried glance at his mother's tear-stained face before he and Pablo were pushed through the side door and out of the courtroom.

Chapter Eight

The following morning Jeffrey and Pablo were ordered to a new facility to await sentencing. Late that afternoon, they were walked through a pouring rain and herded onto a prison transport bus with twenty other convicts, hardened men guilty of serious crimes. The suits and ties the boys wore to court were gone, replaced with orange prison jumpsuits. Like the other twenty prisoners, their wrists were cuffed in front of their body and attached to a belly chain around their waist and their ankles were shackled. They felt like animals being led to slaughter.

The prisoners were separated from the bus driver by a wire mesh partition. A transport guard, holding a shotgun, sat behind the partition, close to the driver. A police cruiser trailed behind the bus, accompanying them to the new facility.

Despite the downpour and overcast sky, traffic heading out of downtown Los Angeles was heavy and moving fast. The bus was silent, save for the hammering of the rain on the roof and the swipe of the windshield wipers. One windshield wiper was broken. Its rubber surface swooshed to the left and smudged to the right.

Jeffrey looked out the window. He had hoped to use this ride as a last glimpse of freedom, of life beyond the bars of a prison cell, but the windows were fogged and he could hardly see. The headlights of approaching cars were blurry beams in the darkness. His thoughts turned inward.

The trial was a hazy nightmare in the recesses of his mind. Only a few images remained clear in his memory: the prosecutor's smug smile when the verdict was read, his father's disbelieving look, his mother's anguished face, and Marisol's defiant stance. She was brave to do that. He wished he could see her now, but he knew the likelihood of his ever seeing her again was slim to none. Instead, he would have to hold her memory. Over time the memory would fade, so he would have to fight to keep it. How Marisol looked, how she talked ... he would picture it to himself every day and run it over and over in his mind. It would become part of his daily ritual, along with his pushups and his prayers. Next to his prayers, it would be the most important thing he could do to maintain his sanity in such an insane situation.

The rain was coming in sheets now, thumping heavily on the bus roof and windshield. Jeffrey continued to think of Marisol. He wondered what she was doing at this very instant. He wondered if some place right now she was looking at the rain and thinking of him and Pablo.

A truck passed. Its rear wheels sent up an arc of spray and drenched the left side of the bus, including Jeffrey's window, and then the truck swerved into their lane. The driver of the prison bus slammed the brakes. Jeffrey and the other inmates lurched forward in their seats with an eruption of shouts.

The bus swayed one way and then the other. Jeffrey heard the frightened shouts of the inmates, the rattle of their chains and shackles, and then he felt a violent jolt as the bus was rammed from behind by another vehicle. The bus driver spun the wheel, fighting for control. Inmates hollered. Jeffrey caught one glance of Pablo, gripping his seat and bracing for impact, and then with a tremendous groan the left side of the bus tilted high and rolled over.

Jeffrey was thrown from his seat. Windows shattered and glass fragments flew everywhere. Jeffrey heard shouts and cries for help all around him. He saw Pablo's body hurtling over his own, and then his head thumped against the wall and everything went black.

The bus rolled twice, slammed to a stop, and bounced on its axils. For a moment all was silent. The screams of the men had stopped and the pelt of the rain on the roof of the bus seemed extra loud. Jeffrey lay crumpled on the floor of the bus, his skull pounding. He opened his eyes. Men around him began to moan.

Jeffrey tried to move and shards of broken glass fell from his hair. He smelled oil and grease and gasoline and the stench of burning rubber. The overhead lights sputtered and shut off.

His glasses were askew. With his handcuffs shackled to his belly chain, he had to bring his legs up in order to reach and straighten them. The hinge on his glasses was bent and they fit crooked on his nose. He saw instantly that the wire mesh partition separating the inmates from the driver and transport guard was mangled and torn. Pablo, with cuts on his face and with his forehead bleeding badly, was slipping through the opening.

Jeffrey watched his friend climb over the body of the dead bus driver, grip the steering wheel and kick out the remainder of the cracked windshield. He heard Pablo say, "Come on, Jeffrey," and watched as Pablo crawled out the windshield onto the wrinkled hood of the bus.

Jeffrey rose slowly to his knees. Every bone in his body rattled with pain. He crawled over the bleeding body of an inmate and squeezed his way through the mangled metal partition. The prison transport guard lay dead on the floor with a broken neck, his mouth and eyes open, his shotgun on the floor next to him. Jeffrey slid his hand into the dead man's pocket and pulled out a large set of keys. In the distance, a police siren whined through the rain.

Pablo whispered hoarsely from the hood of the bus, "Jeffrey, come on." When he saw Jeffrey fumbling with the keys, his eyes opened wide. "You got the keys!"

Jeffrey slid one key after another into the lock on his handcuffs. A small L-shaped key slid in easily and popped the lock on his left cuff. He did the same quickly with the right. Seconds later his belly chain and ankle cuffs were off and he flung them aside. He climbed over the dead body of the bus driver and crawled out the windshield and into a cold gray curtain of rain.

Pablo scooted aside and brought his wrists forward and Jeffrey went to work with the keys. He unlocked Pablo's handcuffs, his belly chain, and his ankle cuffs, and turned back to the interior of the bus. A black prisoner crawled up the middle aisle of the bus, bloodied, but alive. Jeffrey threw him the keys, and then he and Pablo slid off the hood of the bus and onto soft grass. Their prison jumpsuits were soaked and clung to their bodies.

The afternoon sky was dark as night, but they could see they were at the foot of a small embankment. A small crowd was gathered atop the hill, watching. The police cruiser that had been trailing the bus was smashed and sitting nearby atop railroad tracks. When the bus first began to skid, it was the police car that had rammed into it from behind. Jeffrey and Pablo ran to it.

Pablo reached the car first. Steam hissed from the hood. The front end of the vehicle was caved in, along with the driver's side door. The policeman behind the wheel was wedged in behind the wreckage, his bald head covered in blood and his eyes closed. When Jeffrey pulled up, Pablo nodded at the policeman and said, "Is he dead?"

Jeffrey leaned against the car, panting, and looked at the driver. The man looked dead. Jeffrey saw a wedding ring on the man's left index finger and a wave of frustration swept over him. He tried the door, but it wouldn't open. His head was spinning from the accident and the pounding beat of the rain and he took a shaky step back. He tried to think, but his mind clouded over and he felt a panic rising in his body. Laughter and shouts came from behind.

The boys turned to see six olive-skinned Salvadoran men dressed in flannel shirts and khakis descending the small hill. Rain pelted their shaved heads and dripped from their chins and ears. They swept down the hill and headed towards the two boys. The police siren continued to wail in the distance.

Jeffrey's mind was so filled with pounding blood, he froze. Within seconds, the men were at his side, their shoes crunching across the gravel that flanked both sides of the railroad tracks. One of the men, broad-faced and darker than the others, looked to be their leader. A spider web tattoo began at the man's nose and spread over his face, covering everything but his cold, black eyes. Jeffrey had never seen a more terrifying man.

He heard one of the others address this man as Alberto and motion to the police car. Alberto stepped past the boys and went directly to the vehicle. He lowered his head, cupped his hands to the side of his tattooed face and peered inside at the trapped driver.

A third man, thin and gangly, sidled up to the boys, looked them both up and down, and grinned through crooked teeth.

Alberto turned away from the car. He eyed Pablo's bloody face, then turned to Jeffrey and said, "You're a cop killer, boy."

Jeffrey stared back at the man.

"We didn't kill him," Pablo said.

"Tell it to the judge," said one of the men, and the others laughed.

A groan came from the car. Jeffrey and Alberto stared at each other for a moment. Jeffrey stepped past the man to the car and looked inside. The policeman pinned behind the wheel turned his head feebly and gazed up at Jeffrey with pleading eyes. Blood dribbled down his forehead.

Jeffrey shouted, "He's alive."

A train whistle shrieked.

All eyes turned to the sound. At first they saw nothing, only empty tracks that disappeared in the mist and rain. The whistle shrieked again and then they saw it: the outline of an approaching train at the far end of the tracks, hazy yellow orbs for headlights.

"Not for long," said the man with crooked teeth.

Jeffrey turned to Alberto. "We have to get this car off the tracks."

"For what, homie?" said the man with crooked teeth. "He was taking you to jail."

The police siren whined louder and was joined by two others; all three converging from different directions. Alberto stepped closer to Jeffrey, his flannel shirt buttoned up tight against a thick neck. Jeffrey caught the whiff of stale beer on the man's breath and his nostrils pinched. Alberto eyed Jeffrey's crooked glasses, the glass fragments in his hair, and his prison jumpsuit. He said, "You better run, boy."

"We can't leave that policeman here to die," Jeffrey said.

The train whistle shrieked.

Jeffrey and Pablo broke for the car and scrambled around it, trying all the doors.

The men stepped closer. "You ain't getting him out of there," one of them said. "He's trapped behind that wheel."

Alberto made a sharp, sweeping motion with his arm. "Get away from the car."

The men backed away.

"We have to get him out," Pablo shouted. He picked up a rock and drew his arm back to smash the car window. Alberto stepped forward, grabbed Pablo by the front of his jumpsuit and hurled him away from the car. Pablo stumbled across the grass. Alberto barked an order in Spanish and two men grabbed Pablo, pinning his arms.

Alberto turned to Jeffrey. "Did you hear me, boy?"

Jeffrey pointed to the car, his hand trembling. "If we don't get this car off the tracks, that man is going to die."

Anger flashed across Alberto's face. His fist lashed out in the rain. Jeffrey ducked and caught the blow behind his ear. It hit like a sledgehammer. He staggered back and fell in the wet mud. Rain splattered the ground around him.

Jeffrey fought to clear the pounding in his head. He couldn't think, he couldn't see. He straightened his glasses and saw Alberto standing over him, rain streaming down his face. Lightning flashed and Alberto's jawline and the bony ridge of his brow stood out in the glare. "He's a cop," Alberto shouted, "let him die!"

Jeffrey scuttled backwards in the mud and rose shakily to his feet. "We can't do that."

Alberto reached into the back pocket of his khaki pants and pulled out a switchblade knife. He eyed Jeffrey, nostrils flaring, and flicked the blade open.

Pablo shouted, "Run, Jeffrey!"

Jeffrey backed away, white-faced, blood roaring in his ears. He saw the glistening blade of the knife and the fierce, tattooed face of the man holding it. He heard the train whistle screaming, the police sirens wailing louder and louder, and Pablo's shouts.

Alberto stepped closer through the rain, circling the knife in a smooth figure eight. "I'm going to cut you to pieces right now."

Jeffrey pointed to the car. "That man is married, he probably has kids. If he dies, those kids will grow up without a father."

Alberto stopped and Jeffrey saw a flicker in his black eyes.

"Go look for yourself," Jeffrey shouted. "He's wearing a wedding ring."

Alberto's eyes flickered again. As if against his own will, he turned and stepped briskly to the police car. The others watched as he cupped his hand to the side of his face and peered through the driver's side window. His eyes went to the wedding ring on the policeman's finger.

The train whistle shrieked. Alberto looked up. The train was a hundred yards away and closing fast through the rain. Alberto snapped the blade closed, slipped the knife back into his pants pocket and barked an order in Spanish. The men ran to the car and surrounded it. Jeffrey and Pablo joined them. Jeffrey stood next to Alberto on the passenger side of the car, the two of them with their feet planted on the tracks. The others were spread out over the front, back and opposite side of the car. They felt a rumbling under their feet, a pulsing throb on the gravelly surface of the earth from the weight of the approaching train on the tracks.

Alberto shouted, "Uno, dos, tres," and they all heaved. The car moved an inch.

The train whistle screamed through the rain.

"Uno, dos, tres!"

Again they all heaved. The car moved another inch.

The train was forty yards away, whistle shrieking.

"Uno, dos, tres!"

The car moved a foot, its tires scraping against the tracks.

"Uno, dos, tres!"

The train was almost on them. It looked huge now, a screaming metal monster, barreling towards them in the rain. Jeffrey and Alberto were still on the tracks, their faces covered in sweat. The others were off the tracks. Pablo ran around the car and stood next to Jeffrey. They gripped the car with all their might.

"Uno, dos, tres!"

Six men and two boys heaved. The car tires scraped up and over the iron rail and cleared the tracks. Jeffrey, Pablo and Alberto stepped off the tracks with the car and pressed their bodies flush against it. A tremendous rush of wind swept over them and the train roared past behind them, whistle blaring.

Jeffrey's jumpsuit billowed out behind him. He felt the passing train clipping the fabric. A millimeter further back and the train would be ripping his body to pieces. He grimaced, holding every muscle rigid, not daring to move or breathe. Forty seconds passed, forty seconds that seemed like an eternity, but the train finally whooshed past and barreled on down the tracks.

Pablo and the men slumped against the car, exhausted, but alert. The man with crooked teeth whistled loudly with relief and wiped his brow. The others laughed.

Jeffrey fell to his knees at the side of the tracks. He felt his stomach retching. Hot putrid liquid rushed up from his abdomen to the base of his throat. He hunched forward and opened his mouth to vomit, but nothing came out. The burning liquid lodged in his throat.

The police sirens wailed louder, closing in from all directions. Alberto grabbed Jeffrey by the back of his jumpsuit and pulled him to his feet. He turned to Pablo and said, "You, both of you. Come quickly."

Chapter Nine

An electic razor hummed. Men laughed. Jeffrey watched as his hair fell in clumps onto a sheet that was clipped around his neck and covered his upper body.

He sat with his glasses off in a wooden chair in the center of a dimly lit living room somewhere in East Los Angeles. He had a bruise and swelling behind his left ear where Alberto's punch had landed and when the razor ran over the bruise he winced.

Three of the Salvadoran men sat in a sofa across from him. They drank beer out of cans and watched while the man with crooked teeth shaved Jeffrey's head with an electric razor. Alberto sat to the side in a cushy arm chair with a lit cigarette in one hand and a can of beer in the other. Behind him, an open doorway led from the living room to the rest of the house. Beads hung from the top of the doorway down to knee level. Pablo sat on the floor in front of the sofa. Dried blood matted his forehead and face.

The man with crooked teeth finished with the electric razor and reached for a can of shaving cream. He sprayed a glop of the cream into the palm of his hand and rubbed it over Jeffrey's head. Then he picked up a straight razor and carefully shaved away the stubble. When he finished, he ran his hand over Jeffrey's smooth, naked skull, grinned and spoke to the others in Spanish. The men burst out laughing.

Jeffrey looked at Pablo. "What did he say?"

"He said your honorary gang name is Cue Ball."

The men laughed again.

The man with crooked teeth handed Jeffrey a small mirror. Jeffrey put his glasses on, lifted the mirror and saw himself staring back with a bald head. His startled expression brought another round of laughter from the men.

Alberto smiled. "The cops won't recognize you now, Cue Ball." There was more laughter and then a pause as beer cans tilted and the men all took a long pull.

Alberto set his beer on a table at his side, turned to the doorway behind him, and called loudly, "Nancy."

The man with crooked teeth took the mirror from Jeffrey and removed the sheet from around his neck. Another man heaved himself off the couch and hobbled across the room to a stereo system. He fiddled with the knobs and Salvadoran hip hop music filled the room. Moments later the floor was jolted with three sharp raps from below. Jeffrey leapt out of the chair.

"Relax, Cue Ball," said the man with crooked teeth. "It's the old lady downstairs. When we get loud, she beats on her ceiling with a broom handle." He bent down low, his mouth close to the floor, and shouted an insult in Spanish. Three loud bumps from below followed. The men laughed.

"Nancy!" Alberto called to the hallway again.

The beads in the doorway parted and a barefoot Salvadoran girl with smooth brown legs stepped into the room. The girl saw Jeffrey first and then Pablo and took a startled step back. She was wearing shorts and a sleeveless T-shirt and the sight of the two strange boys made her cover her body with her hands. She looked to be their age or younger.

Alberto spoke to the girl in Spanish, but she gave no indication that she heard him. "Nancy!" he snapped. She turned to him. He spoke to her harshly. She lowered her head, turned on her heel, and stepped back through the curtain of beads, disappearing down the darkened hall.

Alberto put his lit cigarette in the corner of his mouth, turned to Pablo and snapped his fingers. Pablo looked up. Alberto jerked his thumb back towards the doorway, an indication for Pablo to follow the girl.

Pablo hopped to his feet and stepped through the beads into the hallway. Behind him, music and laughter spilled from the living room. Ahead of him, a single light shone from a room near the end of the hall. He stepped towards it, the wooden floor creaking under his feet. The scent of grilled pork chops and lima beans from a dinner earlier in the evening hung in the air and grew stronger as Pablo neared the light. He found the girl waiting for him there in the kitchen.

A chair was propped up against the sink; it's back leaning against the counter. The girl stood nearby, her head tilted down and her face hidden behind strands of dark hair. She tore open a plastic bag filled with cotton balls and pointed to the chair.

Pablo sat in the chair and stole a glance at the girl. In the dim light of the kitchen, her skin seemed to glow. She sensed his eyes upon her and turned her face away. Pablo settled back in the chair and gazed up at the ceiling. The girl stepped close to his side and he heard a small gasp.

"You have a cut," she said.

He watched her hand reach high and open a cabinet above the sink. From the cabinet, came a small brown bottle.

"What's that?" Pablo asked.

"Shhh." She opened the brown bottle with a serious face. "Close your eyes."

Pablo obeyed. He waited. Seconds later he felt the cold swab of antiseptic brush across the cut on his forehead, up and then down again, the coldness changing suddenly to burning. His eyes flew open. He wanted to scream and leap from the chair. The girl's hand on his shoulder stopped him. "Close your eyes," she said.

His breath was coming in gasps, but he did what she said. She pressed his shoulder and squeezed. His breath slowly steadied. It was several minutes before her hand left his shoulder and he heard the tear of paper, felt a bandage being placed over his cut, its ends smoothed down by the girl's steady fingers.

He heard the sound of running water and opened his eyes. The girl held a cotton ball under the faucet. She turned to him with a determined expression and used the cotton ball to dab the blood and cuts that speckled his face. First one cotton ball and then another. The cold liquid felt refreshing on his skin. When water trickled down the side of his chin, she used her pinky to wipe it off. Finished, she threw the cotton balls in the trash and washed her hands in the sink.

"You look better now," she said.

"How bad was the cut?"

"Bad. And I've seen some bad ones. You really should see a doctor." She reached for a bottle on the counter.

"What's that?"

"For your hair," she said. "I'm going to make you blond."

Pablo sat up straight. "Blond?"

"Would you rather they shaved you bald, like your friend?"

Pablo shook his head. "Blond, it is."

Music played in the living room. Alberto and three of the men sat at a table, playing poker and drinking beer. Jeffrey and Pablo sat on the sofa and studied each other's appearance, one blond, the other bald.

"What do you think?" Pablo said.

"I don't think it will fool anyone we already know," Jeffrey said, "but it might make it harder for the police to spot us."

The man with crooked teeth pulled up a chair and sat across from them. He handed them each a pair of khaki pants, a flannel shirt, a belt, and a flip phone. "Those are burners," he said, nodding at the phones. "They're hard to trace, but not impossible. Use it and lose it."

The boys nodded and thanked him. Pablo saw Jeffrey staring intensely at the phone in his hand and said, "What's up?"

"I was just thinking, the bus accident was three hours ago, they probably don't know we're missing yet."

The man with crooked teeth nodded in agreement. "It's gonna take them all night to clean up that mess. They won't get a head count till morning."

Jeffrey said to Pablo, "Once the police discover we're missing everyone we know will be under surveillance, with their phones tapped and their emails monitored. But right now there might be a small window of opportunity for us to contact somebody before that happens."

The man with crooked teeth nodded his approval.

"Our parents?" Pablo said.

Jeffrey shook his head. "That was my first thought, but the police and the FBI probably tapped their phones before they even arrested us. Their lines could still be tapped."

"Marisol?"

"She testified at the trial. Her line could be tapped too."

"Susie? She wasn't at the trial and she has her own phone."

Jeffrey thought for moment. "Once the police find out we're on the loose, they'll tap her phone for sure. But right now it could be clear. It's risky. If her line is tapped, they'll know we called her and it could lead to us getting caught." He paused and said, "I think it's a chance we have to take."

The man with crooked teeth nodded again.

Jeffrey dialed a number on his phone. Susie answered and he said softly, "Do you recognize my voice?"

Pablo heard a shriek come from Jeffrey's phone.

Jeffrey cupped the phone with his hand and spoke into it quietly. "Calm down."

"Where are you?" Susie asked.

"I can't tell you. We escaped."

"Escaped, how?"

Jeffrey heard a rustling sound and a faint voice in the background with Susie. His entire body tensed and two thoughts flashed instantly across his mind. First, if Susie's parents were with her and they knew she was talking to him, he would have to hang up and never call back. Second, if the police already knew that he and Pablo were missing, they might already be at Susie's house. He spoke sharply into the phone, "Who's with you?"

"It's okay," Susie said. "It's Marisol."

Jeffrey's eyes flashed. Just hearing Marisol's name sent a deep longing through his body. If he could just hear her voice ... He felt a nudge from Pablo and turned to him.

"We need money," Pablo said.

The man with crooked teeth nodded.

Jeffrey spoke into the phone. "Susie, listen, I hate to ask, but we need money badly."

"How much?"

"Anything at all, anything you can spare."

"I might have some, but how do I get it to you? Are you coming here for it?"

"No, we can't do it in person, it's too dangerous. We'll do it this way: Go to the library in Koreatown, the one close to Western Avenue. Go to the Young Adult section and find the book *1984* by George Orwell. Put the money inside the book, on page 84. If the book's not there, then put it inside a Hemingway book: *For Whom the Bell Tolls* or *A Farewell to Arms*. They can't all be checked out. Don't wait for us or try to find us, it's too risky."

"What if someone finds the money before you do?"

"Then we're out of luck."

"I could wait for you there."

"No, I said no. It's too risky and if you get caught you'll be in serious trouble. I mean it. Tomorrow's Saturday. Go there first thing in the morning, right when they open, and don't tell anyone we talked."

"Can I call you at the number you're using?"

"No, don't even try it. While you're at the library, use the guest computer and set up an email account at the same place you're using now. Use your name, Susie Norris, spelled backwards. Be sure to use the guest computer so you don't have to use your library card. And use a guest computer to check your emails on that account too. We'll communicate that way."

"Hold on," Susie said.

There was another rustling sound over the phone and then a voice said, "Jeffrey?" It was Marisol.

Jeffrey felt a strange lump in his throat. "Yes."

He could hear the relief in her voice. "Thank God. Where are you?"

"Actually, I don't know. We were on a bus, it overturned on the freeway and we managed to get out."

Marisol gasped. "Are you okay?"

"For the most part."

"Wait." There was a pause and when Marisol came back to the line her voice was low and warning. "Susie's parents are here, we have to go. Is Pablo there?"

"Yeah, he's here with me. Hold on."

Jeffrey held the phone out to Pablo. "It's Marisol."

Pablo took the phone and spoke into it quietly.

The man with crooked teeth tapped the side of his skull and pointed at Jeffrey. "You'll go far in the criminal world, Cue Ball."

"Thanks, but we're not criminals. We just want to stay alive and stay out of jail. We're innocent, you know."

"Sure you are."

"No, really we are."

The man with crooked teeth held up his hand. "You don't have to explain it. I know it already. In jail the first thing you learn is everybody is innocent."

Pablo paused in his conversation with Marisol, and shot a quick embarrassed look at Jeffrey and the man with crooked teeth. Then he lowered his voice and whispered into the phone, "I feel the same way about you."

"Homie's got a girl," said the man with crooked teeth.

It was after midnight when Pablo felt a nudge on his shoulder and stirred from his sleep. He and Jeffrey were curled up on the floor in a corner of the living room. Around them, snoring men occupied the sofa and chairs. Nancy was kneeling at Pablo's side, her young face etched with concern and framed by soft, dark hair.

"You have to go," she whispered.

Pablo leaned up on an elbow and rubbed the sleep from his eyes. "What time is it?"

"Never mind the time, just go. It's not safe for you here."

"I thought it was okay to spend the night."

Nancy shook her head. "They're your friends now, because they're drunk and they helped you escape, but tomorrow they'll change. They'll wonder if the police will follow you here, and they'll wonder what you'll tell the police once you get caught. The easiest solution to both of those problems is to kill you."

"Are you serious?"

Nancy nodded solemnly. "That's who they are. You have to go now, while they're asleep. If they knew I told you, it would be bad."

"Bad for who?"

"Bad for you. Very bad for me."

"Are you leaving too?"

Nancy lowered her eyes.

Pablo said, "If it's dangerous here then come with us."

"I can't." She placed a hand on her stomach, just below her belly button. "I'm having his baby."

"Whose baby?"

"Alberto's."

Pablo studied the girl's face. "How old are you?"

"Fourteen."

"That's not right."

"Just go. Please. Before it's too late."

Pablo shook Jeffrey awake and told him the news. Jeffrey was instantly alert. "We better go," he said.

Quickly and quietly, they stripped off their prison jumpsuits and changed into the clothes the man with crooked teeth had given them. They shoved their only possessions, the burner phones they were given, into their pants pockets and carried their jumpsuits. Nancy led them from the living room through the beads, down the long hall and past the kitchen to a door at the end. She held a finger to her lips for silence and opened the door quietly. Outside were wooden steps leading down to a dark alley. "Go now," she whispered.

"How can we help you?" Pablo said.

Nancy shook her head. "You don't have to help."

"I wish we could," Pablo said. "I'm sorry." He placed a hand on the side of her head and brushed her hair gently. Then he and Jeffrey stepped out the door and started down the rickety steps. They were only halfway down when Pablo stopped and turned, hoping to catch a last glimpse of the girl whose warning might be saving their lives, but the door was closed and locked and the lights in the house were all out.

Chapter Ten

The rain had stopped, but the streets were slick and wet and covered in a fine mist. The boys dumped their orange jumpsuits into the newest sewer. Unsure of their bearings or even where they were, they walked west.

It was an odd sensation to be walking free late at night after weeks of captivity with open space all around. Cars passed them so they kept a watchful eye for police vehicles. They reasoned that the accident with the prison bus was probably still being cleaned up, but if the police stopped them for curfew and asked for their ID, they were in big trouble. If that happened, they decided they would each run in a different direction. One of them would likely get caught, but the other would escape.

They found their way to Wilshire Boulevard and continued walking west. Traffic was heavier now. A siren wailed behind them and they both jumped, but it was an ambulance. It sped past, red lights flashing. They walked a mile down Wilshire Boulevard before Pablo spotted a police car approaching their way.

"Cop car," he whispered to Jeffrey. "Look older. Walk older."

"How do I walk older?"

"I don't know, just do it."

Jeffrey removed his glasses, thinking it might make him less recognizable, and slipped them into his shirt pocket. Then he did his best to walk with a confident stride. The police car cruised their way and slowed to get a good look at them. Jeffrey flinched and felt his pulse quickening. The police car seemed about to stop, then sped forward and disappeared down the street.

"That was close," Pablo whispered.

Jeffrey removed his glasses from his shirt pocket. His hands were shaking as he slipped them back on. Pablo noticed and placed a hand on his shoulder. "You did good."

They kept walking. An hour later they found themselves at MacArthur Park. The once beautiful park, with its serene lake and majestic view of downtown Los Angeles, had long ago degenerated into a gang and drug-infested hellhole; a hotbed of violence and crime with an ever present stench. Bodies were often found floating in the lake, and once when they drained the water, hundreds of handguns were found at the lake's bottom, each one a murder weapon quickly disposed. The boys debated whether it was safe to remain there. They decided most likely it wasn't, but they were too tired to go on.

They found a tree whose thick branches had shielded its base from the rain, creating a small dry spot. Pablo kicked away an empty vodka bottle and they sat down with their backs against the tree. Jeffrey estimated the time to be three o'clock in the morning. "You can sleep," he said. "I'll keep watch."

Pablo curled up and fell instantly asleep. Jeffrey's tiredness pulled on him like a weight. He wanted badly to sleep, to forget about the events of the day and of the last several weeks, but sleep was a luxury he couldn't afford. He kept his eye out for the gang members who inhabited the park and assaulted trespassers. He heard a faint scream from the far end of the park. He tensed and turned to the sound and saw a figure running in the darkness, but nothing more.

For the first time he became aware of the chilly night air. A gust of wind blew sharply over his bare skull and sent a shudder down his neck and spine. The top of his head had never felt a sensation like that before. He buttoned his flannel shirt up to his neck and shivered against the cold.

The smog of the city obliterated any view of the stars, but the moon hung full and heavy in the black sky. Its light shimmered on the lake's surface. Jeffrey gazed at the moonlight's reflection on the water and then up at the lights of the tall office buildings around him. He wondered what was going on behind those lights, shining so bright at three o'clock in the morning.

He kept his eyes open and he listened and he thought about his situation. He and Pablo were fugitives now, convicted of murder. One slip and it was off to prison for the rest of their lives. The court proceedings had shown him a side of life that he always knew existed, but had never completely experienced before: the utter corruption of the adult world. So that was how life worked. Now he knew.

He remembered the words of Father Pat, the old neighborhood priest, who once told him that adversity and pain were wake-up calls from God. The more serious the adversity, the priest had insisted, the more the person experiencing it had drifted away from God and needed to change course. "Without adversity," Father Pat had said, "most people would never change". Jeffrey wondered if that was happening to him now. Was it his selfishness that brought him to this point? He had no other explanation. One thing he knew: he wasn't the same person he was before.

Time passed. The darkness dissipated. Jeffrey watched as the sky grew brighter and dawn broke over the city. The day was being born. And so was he.

"The safe way to play this is to split up," Jeffrey said.

He and Pablo stood on the corner of Wilshire Boulevard and Serrano Avenue, not far from the neighborhood library. They had spent the early morning at MacArthur Park, watching it be overtaken by an army of ducks and squirrels. They waited for the streets to fill with traffic and pedestrians, and then walked three miles west down Wilshire Boulevard, past buildings and shops and sidewalks covered with tents, to Koreatown. Some of the homeless tents and shelters they passed were huge, like fortresses. Several police cars had passed them, but not one had stopped or even slowed down. They chalked it up to their altered appearances. It was now close to noon.

"That way if one of us gets caught," Jeffrey continued, "the other can still get away."

Pablo nodded and said, "Maybe I should go then, and you wait here."

"Have you been in this library before?"

Pablo shook his head.

"Let me go then," Jeffrey said. "I've been in there, I know my way around. Give me one hour max. If I'm not back by then, it means I was caught. If that happens, take off as fast as you can."

Pablo gave a grim nod. The two boys shook hands and Pablo watched as Jeffrey crossed the street. Jeffrey approached the library from behind, saw that everything looked normal, and walked to the front. Again, everything looked normal. He took off his glasses, slipped them into his shirt pocket, and stepped inside the library.

His vision was blurry, but he made out a police officer standing twenty feet away. Jeffrey flinched. He would have to walk right past the man to get to the main part of the library. Instantly, his mind calculated his choices. He could turn around and walk out, but the cop's eyes were already on him. To turn around now would be a sign of fear and make him immediately suspicious. If he continued, he risked being recognized. He had only a micro-second to make his decision. He kept walking.

The police officer sized Jeffrey up as he approached. Then he looked elsewhere. Jeffrey strode past the man and past several tables filled with children and their adult tutors. He passed a row of patrons seated at the library's reserved computers and turned confidently to the Young Adult Classics section.

He was out of the policeman's sight now and glanced quickly around. A pretty brown-haired girl in her twenties was fifteen yards away next to a cart loaded down with books. She was a library employee and she was shelving the books, not paying any attention to him. The patrons seated at the tables behind him were engrossed in their phones or quietly reading. Nobody was watching, now was the time to make his move.

His leaned in close and his eyes scanned the author names and book titles. He spotted George Orwell's *1984* and pulled the book from the shelf. Quietly, very quietly, he opened the book and turned to page 84. A white envelope was pressed between the pages. He took the envelope, slipped it into his pants pocket, and shelved the book. He turned and walked to the guest computers behind the librarian's desk.

Jeffrey turned on a computer, brought up a major news site, and felt his heart jump when the image at the top of the page was his and Pablo's mug shots. He read the story quickly. Most of the inmates on the bus were dead, a few were injured and taken to the hospital, and three had escaped: Jeffrey, Pablo, and the black prisoner that Jeffrey had thrown the keys to. A massive manhunt was now underway for all of them.

The police officer driving the car that the two boys and six Salvadoran men had moved off the railroad tracks was alive and doing well. His name was Peter Wingate and he credited the two escaped boys with saving his life. That part of the story was buried at the very end of the article.

Jeffrey checked a few more sites. The bus accident was the top story on every one, with the police asking for the public's help in finding the escaped inmates and offering a reward for any news leading to their capture.

Jeffrey's heart was pounding now. He created a quick email account using his name spelled backwards and sent an email to Susie's new account: *Got it! Thank you!* Then he looked to see if the policeman standing by the front entrance was watching him. He saw the officer strolling toward the checkout desk. The pretty brown-haired girl that Jeffrey saw earlier shelving books was now seated behind the desk. The policeman stopped there and talked to her. Jeffrey turned the computer off and walked quickly toward the main entrance and out of the building.

Outside, he put his glasses back on and saw Pablo sitting by the side of a small grass field facing Wilshire Boulevard. Jeffrey walked past Pablo, across the grass lawn, and sat next to a tree near the middle of the field. Seconds later, Pablo joined him. Both boys kept their backs against the tree and their eyes on the people and the street in front of them.

"You get it?" Pablo asked.

Jeffrey slid the envelope out of his pocket and opened it. The color of green currency immediately caught his eye. There were four twenty-dollar bills inside the envelope. Next to the money was a small note, folded in half. Jeffrey took two of the bills and passed them quietly to Pablo. Pablo glanced quickly at the bills and slipped them into his pocket.

Jeffrey removed the note from inside the envelope and unfolded it. He read it quickly: *This is all the money we have. Where are you? We want to help you. We love you both. Marisol, Susie.*

Jeffrey felt his throat tighten. He read the words again and again and again, and then he passed the note to Pablo.

Pablo read the note and said, "Can I keep this?"

"That's not a good idea."

"Why not?"

"If we get caught and the cops find that note in your pocket, they'll arrest the girls for helping us. They'll go to jail too."

Pablo frowned. For a long moment he sat and stared at the note in his hand. With an anguished face, he tore the note into tiny pieces of paper. He walked across the wide grass lawn to an open wastebasket on the sidewalk and sprinkled the little pieces inside.

Chapter Eleven

The crowded restaurant hummed with mealtime chatter. Silverware clinked against plates and a pair of waitresses bustled about, taking orders and delivering plates of food.

Jeffrey and Pablo sat in the very last booth. Pans rattled from the kitchen close behind them. Jeffrey chewed the final bite of a tender and juicy steak and swallowed it down. After months of jailhouse food, this meal was a sumptuous feast. The Salvadoran men had given him and Pablo some food the night before, but that was seventeen hours ago.

Jeffrey pushed his empty plate to the middle of the table and spoke quietly to Pablo. "The police said Hodges was tied to a chair and tortured with a knife before he was killed. They said that went on for a couple of hours. They also said the killers searched his house and pulled everything out of the drawers and closets and dumped it all on the floor."

"Right," Pablo said. "I remember all of that from the trial."

"To me that sounds like the killers were after something and they tortured Hodges to get him to talk. That's why they searched his house. My guess is Hodges died and didn't tell them what they wanted to hear."

Jeffrey saw Pablo's eyebrows arch high and he continued. "It makes more sense that way. They wouldn't search his place first and then kill him. They would try to get the information they wanted first. If Hodges talks, then they don't have to do any searching. Pulling out all his drawers and emptying his closets is a sign of desperation. What makes more sense is they were after something, but Hodges wouldn't tell them where it was and he died before they could get it out of him. That's when they went to his drawers and closets, looking for what they wanted."

Pablo nodded. "If that's true, then the killers probably didn't find what they were looking for. Because if they did, they would have stopped looking and left, but the police said every drawer and every closet was emptied. That means they searched the entire place and couldn't find what they wanted."

"That's exactly what I'm thinking."

"What do you think they were looking for?"

"That I don't know, but it has to be something worth more than the couple of thousand dollars they spent framing us."

"It also has to be something small enough to fit in a drawer."

"That's a great point, Pablo. I didn't think about that."

"So we're talking money, drugs, jewels, gold, what else?"

"I'd say any or all of the above, or information leading to any of the above."

"It could also be pictures or letters or something that could be used to blackmail somebody."

Jeffrey's eyes glistened. "That's another great point. Now we're getting somewhere. I'll tell you something else. That whole bit about the school security cameras being down when Zinka talked to us in the cafeteria is completely illogical. It was either an accident like everyone said, or it was done deliberately. Which makes more sense?"

"Deliberately."

"Right, and if that's the case, then who could have done it?"

"Popper, Beasley, maybe a few other teachers."

"Who else?"

"You tell me."

Jeffrey paused. "Keller."

"Whoa. You think Keller the janitor is mixed up in this?"

"I know he is, I just don't know how. I also think he helped Brian sneak into school. Do you remember what Beasley told us about the vent that goes from the ceiling in the kitchen to the teacher's lounge? Besides Beasley and Popper, who else would know about that?"

Pablo said, "It would have to be someone who knew how to go from one area of school to another. Probably someone with keys, someone who knows the alarm code. Keller again."

"Right," Jeffrey said. "Remember when Zinka came to our table in the cafeteria? It was the same day we investigated the burglary in the kitchen. She told us everyone in school was talking about it. My ego wanted to believe that, so I did. But after we were arrested I started to think. News travels fast in our school, but not that fast. There were four other people in that kitchen besides us: Brian, Keller, Beasley and Popper. It had to be one of them that told Zinka about us and sent her looking for us in the cafeteria."

"Out of that list, I'd knock off Brian, Beasley and Popper. That leaves Keller. But why would he do that?"

"I'm not sure, but I do know that the center of this entire mystery lies somewhere back at school. That's where it all started.

That's where the burglary in the kitchen occurred. That's where Zinka found us. That's where the cameras were turned off. And that's where Keller is."

"What does it all mean, Jeffrey?"

"It means we have to go back, back to our school. We have to get our hands on whatever files the school has on Keller."

"That's not going to be easy. We could ask Marisol. She was able to get that student roster list, remember? She might be able to get us Keller's file."

"I thought about that. But if she starts poking around for Keller's file and someone at school thinks she's helping us, they'll call the cops and she'll get arrested. It's the same with Susie."

"But we can't do it. If we come within a mile of that school they'll recognize us right away."

"Not if we go at night."

"You mean break in?"

"Not necessarily."

"What are you talking about then?"

"There's one person who can help us. One person who wasn't at the trial and who's probably not under any surveillance right now. One person who can get us inside that school without being seen or getting caught."

"Who?" Pablo waited with an expectant look. Jeffrey merely smiled. Pablo's eyes suddenly flashed. "No way," he said.

"Yes way. It's our only chance."

"Beasley? Are you kidding me?"

"Think about it. He has the alarm code and he's first on the call list. If anything goes wrong he'll get called first and he can talk his way out of it. He just has to turn the alarm off and let us in."

"He won't go for it. And what if he sees us and calls the cops?"

"Then we're in trouble. But he has to know we're innocent. Out of everyone at our school, he has to know. There's only one thing we have to worry about."

"What's that?"

Before Jeffrey could answer, a thump came from the table behind him, followed by the sound of a water glass shattering and a woman's scream. Jeffrey spun around in his seat to see a blond woman leaning out of her booth and gaping in horror at a man dressed in a suit and tie lying sprawled out on the restaurant floor.

Startled diners gasped and turned to look. Jeffrey and Pablo sprang from their seats and kneeled at the man's side. The man on the floor clutched at his chest. He opened his mouth to speak, but no words came out.

Jeffrey's eyes opened wide. "He's having a heart attack."

The blond woman gasped.

Jeffrey turned to Pablo. "Quick, run to the kitchen, get some cayenne pepper."

Pablo jumped to his feet and dashed off. He bumped into a woman with orange dyed hair as she came out of the restroom. Pablo shot a quick look at the woman before he ducked into the kitchen. To his surprise he saw it was Gladys, the cafeteria worker from his school.

Jeffrey turned to the blond woman. "Hand me a glass of water and a spoon." The woman grabbed a water glass and a spoon from her table and passed them to Jeffrey with trembling hands. "Is he going to die?" she asked.

"Not if we hurry," Jeffrey said. "Cayenne pepper will stop a heart attack in its tracks."

He poured half of the water from the glass onto the floor, leaving the glass half full.

A pair of waitresses and a small crowd of diners formed a half-circle around them, filming with their phones. A uniformed security guard stood close by, calling for an ambulance.

Pablo dashed out of the kitchen, holding a shaker of cayenne pepper in his hand. He squeezed his way through the crowd and kneeled next to Jeffrey. Jeffrey took the cayenne pepper, sprinkled two dashes into the half-filled glass of water and stirred it quickly with the spoon. He said to Pablo, "Help me with his head."

Pablo cradled the man's head in his heads and raised it gently from the floor. Jeffrey lifted the water glass to the man's lips and said, "Drink this."

The blond woman watched with a stricken look on her face as the man gulped at the water. With each swallow, a trickle of water spilled out of the corner of his mouth and ran down his chin. Jeffrey lifted the glass higher and higher until all the water was drained. The man's eyes popped open wide.

In the crowd behind them, Gladys nudged a woman standing next to her. "It's them boys from my school," she whispered, "the two killers." Her friend covered her mouth in shock. Gladys pulled a phone from her pocket, punched in three numbers and raised the phone to her ear.

The man on the floor patted his chest, as if searching for something. "It's stopped," he said. The crowd gasped and the blond woman stepped in closer.

Pablo leaned in close to Jeffrey and whispered, "Don't turn around. That lady from the cafeteria, the one with orange hair, she's here. I think she recognized us."

Jeffrey nodded almost imperceptibly. The man on the floor sat up, still patting his chest. "It's gone," he said to the blond woman.

Jeffrey and Pablo stood up. A dozen phones from the crowd turned their way. The blond woman reached for Jeffrey's arm. "You saved my husband's life, how can I ever repay you?"

"Don't worry about it," Jeffrey said, and handed her the shaker of cayenne pepper. "Just get him some of this at a health food store and give him a little every day. It'll clear his circulation." He and Pablo turned to leave.

"Please stay," the woman said. "The paramedics are coming. I want you to tell them about this."

The boys ignored her and slipped past the crowd on their way to the front door

Gladys yelled, "Those boys are killers! Don't let them leave!"

Jeffrey and Pablo pretended not to hear and continued walking towards the door.

"Stop them," Gladys yelled.

The security guard hustled up behind Jeffrey and reached for his arm. Jeffrey jerked his arm loose and he and Pablo broke for the door.

Pablo reached the door first. He yanked it open and turned around. Jeffrey was five yards behind him, the security guard two yards behind Jeffrey. An elderly man sat with his family in the waiting section by the door, his walker in front of him. Pablo grabbed the walker. Jeffrey rushed past him and out the door and Pablo hurled the walker at the feet of the security guard. The guard tripped over the walker and toppled to the floor. The elderly man stared with his mouth hanging open. His family members screamed. Pablo followed Jeffrey out the door.

The boys ran west on Wilshire Boulevard. Pablo had taken the lead and he was in front, striding long, Jeffrey close behind. Jeffrey had lost so much weight he felt like he was flying. Behind them came the sound of running feet, clopping hard on the pavement, and voices crying, "Stop! Stop them!" A crowd waiting for the bus at the corner ahead stood and stared.

The light at the signal ahead of them turned green and they dashed into the street without breaking stride. A motorcycle in the crossing lane ran the red light and swerved to avoid hitting them. The motorcycle slid to the street, spilling its driver, his helmet scraping against the pavement. Onlookers screamed.

Pablo grabbed the cycle and hopped onto the seat. "Jeffrey, get on!"

"My bike," the driver shouted.

"We're just gonna borrow it," Pablo shouted back.

Jeffrey hopped on behind Pablo.

"Wait," the driver shouted.

Directly ahead, a police car was streaming towards them, siren wailing, red and blue lights popping atop its hood. Pablo spun the cycle around. The security guard and two male diners from the restaurant sprinted into the intersection. They reached for the cycle, grasping. It roared past them, just out of reach.

A man ran out into the middle of the street to stop them. Pablo veered the cycle around him and bounced it up onto the sidewalk. People on the sidewalk screamed and dodged out of the way. The cycle zipped past the restaurant where they had eaten, zigzagging left and right to avoid hitting bystanders.

At the next intersection, Pablo weaved the cycle back onto the street. Everywhere, people were shouting, pointing, filming with their phones. Cars in the opposite lane slowed, drivers staring out their windows. The police car was close behind, its siren wailing loud.

Pablo shouted, "Hang on, Jeffrey!" and accelerated. The cycle zoomed ahead. The wind stung Pablo's eyes and he fumbled for control of the bike.

At the intersection of Wilshire and Normandie Avenue, Pablo swung the cycle left, barely missing an oncoming semi-trailer truck. People on the sidewalk screamed. The police car hung the same left turn, tires screeching. A second police car fell in line behind it. Sirens were blaring from all directions now.

Cars, hearing the sirens, pulled over, leaving a clear path. The cycle passed them like sticks on a picket fence. The cycle dipped low with the road and then up. It hit the top of a hill, leapt into the air and came down with a bouncing jolt. Pablo fought the handlebars to keep it upright and raced on. The road dipped again into a valley and then upward to another hill. Pablo accelerated. The cycle swooped down and up. It leapt again into the air, hung suspended for a micro-second, and landed with another jolt.

The police cars were hitting the hills slower and the cycle opened up a lead, but sirens were wailing ahead of them now and soon there would be a helicopter, tracking them overhead and leaving them nowhere to hide.

"We gotta ditch the bike," Pablo shouted. He slowed and swung the cycle onto a side street lined with restaurants and shops. He steered the bike into an alley and braked abruptly. The cycle skid recklessly and rammed into a metal dumpster. The impact threw both boys onto the pavement. For a moment, they lay still. Sirens were wailing, but not as loud as before. They rose shakily. Pablo ran with a limp down the trash-strewn alley. Jeffrey followed.

They stopped at a door and Pablo yanked it open. They stepped through the door and into a hot and steaming restaurant kitchen that smelled of frying peppers. A startled Hispanic cook looked up from the hissing grill. The teenage dishwasher stopped and stared. Jeffrey and Pablo ran past them both, through the kitchen and into the busy dining area. They ran past tables of astonished diners and out the front door to a busy street. Traffic was heavy and cars were parked at all the meters. Sirens blared from all directions.

"We're trapped," Jeffrey said.

Pablo spotted a boy their age sitting in the passenger seat of a car parked at the curb. The driver's seat was empty. "Come on," he said, and ran to the car.

The boy in the car had his head down, engrossed in his phone. Pablo opened the door to the back seat. He and Jeffrey piled inside and scrunched down, hidden from view from anyone on the street.

The boy turned around with alarm. "What are you doing in the car?"

Pablo talked fast. "Dude, we need your help."

"Get out of the car," the boy shouted.

"Do you know who we are?"

"I don't care who you are, get out of my car!"

"Listen, just listen. Please, I'm not kidding. We need help."

The boy surveyed the two intruders and their desperate, pleading eyes. "Help with what?" he said.

"We're the guys in the news, the guys the police are after, but we're innocent. If they catch us they'll lock us away forever."

"You're lying."

"We're not lying. What's your name?"

"Max."

"Max, I'm telling you the truth. We're innocent. We were framed for a murder we didn't commit."

"How do I know you're not lying?"

"Look at us. Do we look like killers to you?"

Max nodded at Jeffrey. "He does."

"Never mind him. Just help us. Please. I'm telling you the truth. If the police catch us, we're dead. We have to get out of this neighborhood."

"What do you want *me* to do?"

"Just let us hide out here. Don't tell anyone."

"Max!"

The voice came from the street. Max turned and saw his mother striding towards the car.

"My mom's coming," he said.

Jeffrey ducked down as far as he could. Pablo said, "Max, we need you, man. Please don't say anything. Remember, our lives are in your hands." He lifted a finger to his lips as a sign not to talk and ducked down with Jeffrey.

Max's mother opened the driver's side door and slid in behind the wheel. She turned to Max, breathless, her face flush with excitement. "Did you hear what happened? Those two boys, the ones who murdered that man and escaped, they're loose in this area."

"Really?" Max said.

His mother slid a key into the ignition. "That's so scary. Imagine, two killers on the loose. They could be anywhere.

Probably right under our noses. I can almost smell them." She sniffed at the air and started the car.

Max stole a glance at the back seat. The boys were hidden, but the slightest sound would give them away.

A police helicopter buzzed overhead. Max's mother looked up and pointed to it. "Ah, there's the helicopter. Those two are trapped. There's no way they're getting away now." She pulled the car away from the curb and drove off.

Max lowered his head and pretended to look at his phone.

His mother eyed him suspiciously. "Have you gained weight?"

Max looked up from his phone. "Not since yesterday."

"This car feels heavy," his mother said, "like we're riding low to the ground."

In the backseat, Jeffrey and Pablo tensed. Max looked at his phone. Ahead of them and on the opposite side of the street, two police cars were parked and several officers were setting up a roadblock. Max's mother slowed the car, rolled down her window and called to the officers, "Good luck! I hope you catch them!"

A towering policeman with a dark mustache waved back. Max's mother rolled up her window and sped off. To Max, she said, "There's a reward out for them, you know."

"Really, how much?"

"Fifty thousand dollars."

Max's eyes widened.

Jeffrey and Pablo listened intently.

Max said, "How do you collect the reward money?"

"Just turn them in," his mother said. "Dead or alive."

Jeffrey twitched.

"It didn't say that!" Max said.

"It could have. Just think, fifty thousand dollars. We could really use that money."

"But how do you know they're guilty?"

"They're guilty," she said emphatically.

"But how do you know?"

"It was all over the news while the trial was going on. If it's on the news it has to be true, right?"

"No way. Don't innocent people go to jail?"

"Sometimes, but not those two. Uh-uh. I saw their pictures. Actually, the good-looking one, him I'm not sure about. They say he's the one who did the actual killing. But that other one? Guilty as sin, I guarantee you."

Jeffrey's nostrils flared.

Max nodded unconvincingly.

His mother glanced at him. "You act like you want them to get away."

"Well, if they're innocent."

"They're not innocent, I told you. Listen, let me tell you something, evil people are like that. They act like they're innocent: 'Oh, please, help me! Help me!' But then when you do, and your back is turned, they loop that piano wire over your neck and strangle you to death."

Max's eye turned ever so slightly to the back seat.

"I'm telling you, I've seen it," his mother said, and she nodded her head for emphasis. "I've seen it. Choked the life right out of them." She made a gagging sound with her throat to illustrate the point. When Max did not respond, she said, "Are you okay? You look a little pale."

"I'm fine. I'm just ... I was thinking about what you said."

"Don't worry about those two. They're dead meat when the police catch them." She turned the wheel.

Max sat up straight. "Wait, where are you going?"

"There's no rain today, I'm getting the car washed."

In the backseat, Jeffrey and Pablo froze.

Max shouted, "No."

His mother looked at him. "What's wrong with you?"

"You're going to get the car washed now?"

"Yes, now."

"But why?"

"I just told you."

"No, don't do that."

"Why not?"

"Just don't."

"What is *wrong* with you?"

"Nothing, but that car wash is a ripoff."

"Since when?"

"Since forever. I can wash the car."

"You?"

Max nodded. "I can do a better job and it'll save money."

His mother laughed.

"I'm serious," Max said.

"Okay." She shook her head and looked at him strangely. "If you say so." She moved the car into the left lane, pulled a U-turn, and guided the car back to its original direction. "I don't know what's gotten into you," she said. "If I didn't know better, I'd say you were hiding those killers yourself."

A short ride later they arrived in their own neighborhood. Max's hands were shaking as the car drove down his street and pulled into the driveway. His mother parked the car, popped open her door and climbed out. Max opened his door, but remained in the car. His mother started up the walk. "Let me know when you're done washing the car," she called over her shoulder.

"Right," he called back. To Jeffrey and Pablo in the back seat, he whispered, "Don't get out yet."

Max climbed out and stood by the car until his mother opened the front door to the house and stepped inside. When the door closed behind her, Max opened the car door to the back seat and said, "All right, get out of here."

"Thank you, man," Pablo said. "Thank you. We owe you."

He and Jeffrey climbed out of the car, shook hands with their rescuer and sprinted off down the street. Max watched as they reached the end of the street and disappeared around the corner.

Chapter Twelve

The loud knock on Mr. Beasley's front door sounded urgent. He was expecting his wife, but she wouldn't be knocking unless she forgot her keys. He hurried to the door, undid the chain lock, slid open the bolt lock, turned the lock on the knob, and swung the door open. He did not recognize the two young men standing before him. Jeffrey's bald head and Pablo's blond hair made them almost unrecognizable. Then their faces registered in his mind and he shouted, "Good heavens!"

"Mr. Beasley, we're in trouble," Jeffrey said.

The teacher grabbed Jeffrey by the arm and pulled him into the entrance hall. Pablo followed. The teacher closed the door behind them, fastened all three locks, and stepped quickly to the adjacent living room. From behind the lace curtains, he pressed close to the window and looked up and down the street.

"Who followed you here?"

"Nobody," Jeffrey said.

"Are you sure?"

"I don't think so. We're innocent."

"I know that, but the police don't. Your pictures are all over the news." Mr. Beasley turned away from the window and gave them each a closer look. "How you used to look, anyway. Those are clever disguises, but what in the world are you going to do now? You can't possibly remain on the run like this."

"That's why we're here," Jeffrey said. He and Pablo stepped from the entrance hall into the living room. "We need your help."

"*My* help?"

"We need a place to hide out for a few days," Pablo said. "And we need your help with something else."

"It's like this," Jeffrey said, and he explained how he and Pablo were framed, their suspicions about Keller, and the conversation they had in the restaurant.

"I follow your line of thinking," the teacher responded, "and it is highly suspicious. I can assure you it wasn't I that disabled those cameras when you spoke to that girl."

"I want a look at Keller's files," Jeffrey said. "I want to examine every piece of information the school has on him."

"And just how do you intend to do that?"

The boys exchanged a look and Pablo said, "You could do it."

"Me?" Mr. Beasley took a step back. "Absolutely not. Now listen, I would if I could, to help you, of course. But there are too many people flittering around that administration office. I couldn't possibly get my hands on somebody's file without being seen."

"You have keys," Jeffrey said. "You could do it early in the morning before anyone arrives."

"Yes, and then I'm on the security cameras, pilfering a file. Granted, it's unlikely that anyone will see the footage, but there I am. If it ever came up, I would be ruined."

"Then we'll have to do it," Jeffrey said.

"Who is 'we'?"

"Me and Pablo. With your help, of course."

Mr. Beasley narrowed his eyes. "What do you mean with my help?"

"We need you to help us sneak into school tonight."

"Sneak into school? Are you out of your minds?"

"Maybe," Pablo said.

"We have to go back," Jeffrey insisted. "Don't you see? This might be our only chance to prove we're innocent."

Mr. Beasley shook his head. "Out of the question."

"But you have to," Jeffrey pleaded.

"I don't have to do anything, much less assist you in burglarizing a school."

"We're not burglarizing. We're going there to look for clues."

"Remember what you told us last fall," Pablo said, "about treasure hunting? You said when one is on a treasure hunt all propriety goes out the window."

Mr. Beasley scoffed. "Don't tell me what I said or didn't say six months ago. That's all in the past. Besides, this isn't a treasure hunt. It's breaking and entering."

Jeffrey said cautiously, "It's not breaking and entering if a person has permission to enter, and you do."

"Nonsense. You're confusing the issue. I have permission to enter at a precise time on designated school days. I don't have permission to enter at night when the school is closed. On top of all that, you're convicted criminals. Murderers, no less, and you're on the run from the police."

"But we're innocent."

"Yes, I know that." Mr. Beasley sat on the couch, his elbows on his knees and his hands on the sides of his head. "I can see the headlines now: Esteemed Educator and Pillar of the Community Jailed for Helping Escaped Killers Burglarize High School."

Pablo said, "That's crazy."

"This whole scheme of yours is crazy."

"It's our only chance," Jeffrey insisted. "And if you want to get technical, it is like a treasure hunt. Only instead of gold or silver, we're looking for clues. Clues that can prove we're innocent and free us from jail."

"And what if you get caught?"

"Then we're back to jail for the rest of our lives."

"And me along with you."

"You don't have to be there," Pablo said.

Jeffrey echoed Pablo's words: "You don't have to be there, Mr. Beasley. If we get caught, we'll take the blame. We won't mention you at all."

"Famous last words."

"No, really, we mean it. We owe you that much. Besides, the police think we're killers. They'll believe whatever we confess to."

They heard tires crunching on the gravel driveway outside. Mr. Beasley's face blanched white. "It's Mildred!"

A car door slammed outside.

Mr. Beasley leapt to his feet. "Quick, out the back door." He pushed them towards the hallway, leading to the rest of the house.

Pablo turned to him. "What if the neighbors see us?"

Mr. Beasley stopped. "You're right."

Footsteps tapped across the front porch. A key turned in the lock on the front door.

"She's coming in, hide in the closet!" Mr. Beasley turned to the closet in the entrance hall and slid the door open. He shoved the boys inside and whispered, "Don't say a word." He slid the closet door closed.

The front doorknob rattled. The door opened four inches and then snagged on the safety chain. A woman's voice snapped, "Herbert!"

"Coming!" Mr. Beasley stepped quickly to the front door. He pushed the door in, undid the chain lock and stepped back. The door swung open and Mildred Beasley, a small woman with an inquisitive face, stepped inside. She took one look at her husband and said, "What's wrong with you?"

"Wrong? Nothing at all. Why do you ask?"

"You look white as a ghost."

Mr. Beasley took a step back. "Do I? Well, I can't imagine why. I feel fit as a fiddle. Perhaps it's a lack of sunlight. We've had a lot of rain lately, you know."

She eyed him suspiciously and removed her coat. He reached for it.

"Now what?" she said.

"I'll take your coat."

"I'll take it myself," she said, and tried stepping around him to the closet.

He blocked her path and reached again for the coat. "Mildred, please." He yanked the coat out of her hands.

"What is *wrong* with you?"

"Nothing, I told you. I'm just trying to do you a favor and you're showing no appreciation at all."

"I'd appreciate it if you'd act normal," she said. She watched as he stepped to the closet, stopped, and turned back to face her.

"Yes?" he said.

Mildred shook her head and went into the living room. Mr. Beasley opened the closet door a crack. Without looking, he threw the coat inside. The boys were crouched in the darkness. The coat landed on top of Jeffrey and covered his head. Mr. Beasley closed the closet door.

"You heard the news?" Mildred said.

Mr. Beasley joined her in the living room. "What news?"

"Those boys of yours, those killers, they escaped."

"You don't say."

"I do say. They won't be on the run for long though. The police are closing in." She kicked off her shoes and stretched back on the sofa. "If I was the judge, I'd sentence them both to hang."

In the closet, Jeffrey and Pablo both stiffened.

"Did you know," Mildred said, "that when they hang you for murder it takes place in the morning? First, they strap your hands behind your back. Then they lead you down the long corridor to the execution chamber. From there, you have to climb exactly thirteen steps up to the gallows where they put a black hood over your head. Then—"

"Mildred, please."

"I'm just telling you the facts."

"I've heard enough."

"I haven't got to the good part yet."

"I have no desire to hear the good part."

"Well, if hanging's too much for you, how about the electric chair?"

"I have no desire to hear about the electric chair either."

"Why not?" She balled her hand into a fist and shook it. "I'd pay money to see those boys of yours fry in the electric chair.

Especially that snobby one who thinks he knows everything. One throw of the switch and his flesh would sizzle like a steak on a barbeque grill."

In the closet, Jeffrey's eyes widened.

"Mildred, you're being melodramatic."

"Not at all. The Catholic Church has always recommended the death penalty for heretics and murderers. It's been that way forever, nothing has changed."

"Yes, if the party is guilty."

"You're saying they're not?"

"I'm saying there's an abundance of reasonable doubt."

"Baloney. Their fingerprints were all over the crime scene and the murder weapon. And what about the money they found? The police found money on those boys with consecutive serial numbers from money at the victim's home."

"I'm sure there's a logical explanation for everything you've described."

"You bet there is: murder."

"I don't understand how you can be so distrustful. You served them each tea before in this very house. Don't you remember?"

"Of course, I remember. Even then I knew there was something suspicious going on with those two. I'll tell you this, if I see either one of them, I'm calling the police."

"Really? You wouldn't notify me first?"

"Why should I? They may have been nice boys in your class, but that was just an act. Inside, they're killers." She rose and started out of the room.

"Where are you going?"

"To take a bath."

Mr. Beasley watched her disappear down the long hall to the bathroom and waited. Moments later, he heard the sound of water running from the bathtub. He stepped quietly to the closet in the entrance hall, slid the door open, and held a finger to his lips for silence. He took a quick look down the hall. Satisfied that Mildred was not watching, he pulled the boys out of the closet and into the kitchen. He opened a door in the kitchen that led to the garage and motioned the boys through. Then he followed them into the garage and closed the door behind him.

"You'll have to hide in my car until I come for you," he said quietly. "Keep low and out of sight just in case and keep your voices down. No talking, no whispering. And whatever you do, stay put. I'll try to sneak some food out to you after Mildred goes to sleep. Otherwise, don't move until I come for you in the morning."

Mildred called his name from the house. "I'm coming," he called back. To the boys, he said, "Understand? Wait, don't say a word. Just nod your heads." Both boys nodded. "Good. Now get in and keep quiet." He unlocked the car doors and shooed them inside. Jeffrey took the front seat, Pablo the back.

Jeffrey whispered, "What about the school, Mr. Beasley?"

"I already told you, no."

"But we need you. Without your help, we'll be in jail for the rest of our lives."

Pablo whispered, "Please, Mr. Beasley. You're our only hope."

Mildred called from the house, "Herbert!"

Mr. Beasley shouted back, "I said I'm coming!" He turned to the two boys and studied their faces. Their expressions were pleading, haunted, desperate. "Stay put for now," he said. "I'll be back at midnight.

Chapter Thirteen

Crickets chirped. Mr. Beasley pulled his car over to the side of the road and turned the ignition and headlights off. Outside the car windows, the night was inky black with only a sliver of moon. "I'm stopping here," he said, "because I don't want to get too close to the school."

Jeffrey sat in the passenger seat, holding a flashlight. Pablo leaned forward from the back seat, also holding a flashlight.

Mr. Beasley removed a key from his shirt pocket and held it up for Jeffrey to see. "This is the key to the gym door. I made a copy so you don't have to return it to me. Dispose of it when you're finished, some place where nobody will find it." He handed the key to Jeffrey and pulled two more keys connected to a small ring from his pocket. "The first key is the one you requested to access the administration offices, and the other is a master key to all of the classrooms. They're copies, just like with the door key, so I don't need any of them back. Now if you're caught with any of these keys, you'll have to tell the police you stole them before your arrest. That will only incriminate you further, so my advice is don't get caught with them. Got it?"

"Got it," Jeffrey said.

Mr. Beasley turned to Pablo in the back seat.

"Got it," Pablo said.

Mr. Beasley handed the two additional keys to Jeffrey. He took a slip of paper with a row of numbers written on it from his pocket. "This is the alarm code. Input these numbers on the keypad on the alarm panel, directly to your left when you enter from the gym door. Now listen carefully. The second you open the door, you're going to hear a beeping sound coming from the alarm panel. You're also going to see a red light flashing on the panel. Both of those things tell you that the alarm needs to be turned off. You'll have thirty seconds from the time you open the door to turn off the alarm. If more than thirty seconds pass and the alarm isn't turned off, the alarm company will be notified. They'll call me first and I'll have to tell them to dispatch the police. So get that alarm turned off right away. It's the same procedure when you leave. As soon as you enter the code, the panel will begin to beep and the red light will flash. You'll have thirty seconds from the time you set the alarm for you to exit the building and lock the door. Got it?"

"Got it," both boys said.

Mr. Beasley handed the slip of paper to Jeffrey. "Don't get caught with that alarm code either. Now there's nothing I can do about the security cameras. To disable them I would have to call the alarm company and that would be too suspicious, especially this late at night. The good news is nobody is watching those cameras live. The video is saved, but as long as nothing suspicious occurs, no one will ever request the footage and no one will ever see what those cameras record."

Mr. Beasley continued, "It's the same with your fingerprints. They'll be all over the place, but as long as nothing unusual occurs, no one will ever bother to check. Also, you're former students, so it makes sense that your prints will be there.

"Don't waste time. Do what you have to do and get out of there. I'll give you one hour." He checked his watch and tapped it. "It's twelve-thirty. If you're not back by one-thirty, I'll assume something went wrong and leave. The same if I see a police car or hear a siren, I'll assume the worst and leave. If something does go wrong, don't call me or even think about me. I haven't seen either of you since your arrest and we never had this conversation. Got it?"

"Got it."

Jeffrey opened the car door and slid a leg out.

"Jeffrey."

It was the first time Mr. Beasley had ever called Jeffrey by his first name. Jeffrey stopped and turned to face him.

"Good luck," Mr. Beasley said, and extended his hand.

Jeffrey took the teacher's hand and shook. Mr. Beasley's grip was firm and strong.

Mr. Beasley turned to Pablo and they shook hands. Then both boys exited the vehicle, closed the car doors, and walked off.

They walked quickly to the rear of the school, stepping from the darkened street into an area illuminated by floodlights. Jeffrey noticed Pablo limping and said, "You okay?"

Pablo replied tersely, "I'll live." A moment later, he added, "I hurt my knee when we ditched the motorcycle. It's swelling pretty bad."

They reached the twelve-foot chain link fence that surrounded the school. Looking up from the street, the fence seemed a mile high.

"Can you climb okay?" Jeffrey said.

"Don't worry about me," Pablo said. "I'll make it." He stuffed his flashlight into the waistband of his pants, lifted his good leg and inserted the toe of his shoe into a link on the fence, reached up high and pulled his body upward. He proceeded to climb the fence. He stopped at the top to catch his breath, and then hoisted himself over, grimacing in pain as he swung his injured leg over the top of the fence. Jeffrey watched as Pablo climbed down the other side, his face etched in agony. Back on the ground, Pablo bent at the waist, gripped his knee, and nodded at Jeffrey.

Jeffrey climbed quickly, the fence swaying slightly under him. He swung himself over the top and climbed back down the other side. The two boys crossed the flood-lit parking lot to the gym door. Jeffrey slid the key inside the lock and turned to Pablo. "Ready?"

Pablo nodded. Jeffrey turned the key, opened the door and stepped inside. Pablo followed. Inside, everything was dark. They closed the door behind them and locked it and turned immediately to the alarm panel on the wall to their left.

"It's not beeping," Pablo said, "and there's no red light."

Jeffrey stared at the alarm panel with a quizzical expression. "What do we do?"

"I think you better try it anyway."

Jeffrey held the slip of paper with the alarm code written on it and Pablo illuminated it with his flashlight. Jeffrey entered the numbers. Immediately after he pressed the last number, the alarm panel began to beep and a red light atop the panel began to flash.

Pablo said, "This is crazy. Beasley told us it's supposed to go off when we enter the code."

"Unless we just set it," Jeffrey said. He entered the numbers again. The beeping and the flashing red light both stopped. "Okay, I think we just turned it off, which means it wasn't set when we first walked in."

"Are you sure?"

"We'll find out in thirty seconds."

They waited, the seconds passed. The school was silent.

"I guess we did just turn it off," Jeffrey said.

"I don't get it."

"Either someone forgot to set the alarm when they closed up the school, or they did set the alarm, but somebody turned it off later. If that's the case, then whoever turned it off later could be in the building right now."

"Uh-oh."

"Come on, let's get what we came for and get out of here."

They walked quickly to the administration offices. Jeffrey unlocked the door and they stepped inside.

"Leave the light off," Jeffrey said, "just in case there is somebody else besides us in the building."

They stepped behind the front counter that served to separate staff from students. Before them were half-a-dozen desks and the same number of file cabinets. Jeffrey gestured with his flashlight, separating the room in half. "You take that side, I'll take this one. Look for files on Keller, anything you can find."

The boys separated and went to work. They started with the file cabinets, holding their flashlights with one hand and using their other hand to rifle through the files. Pablo finished one cabinet and turned to the next. The file drawers on this cabinet were labeled alphabetically and the fourth drawer down was labeled J-K. The drawer opened with a squeal. Pablo skipped the letter J and went to the back of the drawer to the files beginning with the letter K. He rifled through them and found one with Keller's name on it.

"I got it," he said, and pulled the file out of the cabinet.

Jeffrey was at his side in an instant. The first page in the file was Keller's paper job application dated six months ago. Behind that was a photograph of Keller, along with tax and medical forms he had signed.

Jeffrey scanned the papers. "This is it, this is what we need. We can study it back at Beasley's house." He lifted his shirt, slid the hard manila folder against his bare stomach, and pulled his shirt down over it. He tucked his shirt in and felt the sharp edges of the file folder poke sharply against his skin.

"Jeffrey!" Pablo's voice was low and tense. Jeffrey turned to him. Pablo switched off his flashlight and nodded to the window on the door that led to the hallway. "I saw someone pass by."

Jeffrey turned his flashlight off and they crouched low in the darkness. Minutes passed. Jeffrey tapped Pablo on the arm. He pointed to the open cabinet where Pablo extracted Keller's file. Pablo lifted the drawer slightly to keep it from squealing and slid it closed, then both boys crept to the door. Pablo opened it slowly and peered down both sides of the hallway. He stepped out slowly. Jeffrey followed and quietly closed and locked the door behind him.

Pablo led the way down the hall, stepping lightly across the tile floor, heading back the way they came in. They neared a corner and Pablo reached for Jeffrey's arm. They stopped and listened. Footsteps echoed down the hall behind them.

They turned the corner and walked faster. The footsteps behind them also walked faster. They broke into a run, knowing whoever was behind them could hear them now, but not caring. The footsteps behind them also began to run.

Pablo slid to a stop, opened a door in the hallway to a supply closet and pulled Jeffrey inside. Pablo swung the door almost closed, leaving it open just a crack, and peeked out through the opening. A figure dressed in a hooded sweatshirt and holding a flashlight was running directly towards them.

Pablo whispered in a startled voice, "It's Brian." He took a step back. The door burst open and Brian barreled inside. He bumped into Pablo, who bumped into Jeffrey, and the three of them fell down in a heap. Brian yelled and scuttled backwards in the closet. His flashlight opened bright in Pablo's eyes.

"It's us, man. It's us," Pablo said. He and Jeffrey stood up.

Brian jumped to his feet. "Jones! Reyes! What are you doing here?"

"The same thing you're doing," Pablo said, "hiding." He pushed Brian's flashlight aside so it was no longer shining in his face.

Brian lowered his hood. "You guys almost gave me a heart attack." He gestured towards the hall. "I heard footsteps. I thought someone was following me or maybe it was a ghost."

"We thought the same thing."

"How did you guys get in here?"

"How did *you* get in here?"

"I asked you first. You're supposed to be in jail."

"And you're supposed to be home, sleeping."

"You look different, both of you."

"We escaped," Jeffrey said.

"For real? What are you doing here, hiding out?"

"Looking for clues," Jeffrey said.

"Clues?" Brian laughed. "You guys are innocent, right?"

"What do you think?" Pablo said.

"I didn't follow your trial, but I know you guys have to be innocent." He chuckled. "Jones, I know you didn't kill anyone."

"Then you can answer a few questions," Jeffrey said. "Like how you made a deal with Keller to sneak into school."

Brian laughed nervously. "What are you talking about?"

Pablo took a step forward. "Don't play dumb, man."

Jeffrey reached for Pablo's arm and held him back. To Brian, he said, "We don't have time to play games. We know you made a deal with Keller to sneak into school. Tell us how you did it."

Brian drew himself up. "If you're so smart, you tell me."

"We know what you did," Jeffrey said, "but we don't know how. We know you snuck into the teacher's lounge to steal the answers to Beasley's test. We know it was your footprint we saw on the countertop. We know all of that, so stop pretending like you don't know what we're talking about."

"You figure all that out just now, Jones?"

"From the beginning, only I didn't say anything."

"But you will now, right?" Brian reached in his pocket and pulled out a cell phone. "How about if I call the police and turn both of you in?"

Blood rushed to Pablo's face and he lunged forward. Jeffrey dropped his flashlight and grabbed Pablo from behind just before he reached Brian. Brian jumped back, bumped into a stack of cardboard boxes filled with paper towels and knocked them to the floor. Pablo shook himself free and shouted at Brian, "You turn us in and I'll kill you!"

"You'll be in jail, Reyes."

"I'll kill you before I go to jail!"

Jeffrey placed himself between the two boys. He kept his eyes on Brian, but spoke to Pablo, "Relax, he's not turning anyone in. If he does, he'll have to tell the police he's been sneaking in here at night to steal test answers and he'll go to jail too. Isn't that right, Brian?"

Brian shrugged and slid his phone back in his pocket.

Pablo stepped back and stared at Brian with hate-filled eyes, his hands trembled with rage.

Brian said, "Yeah, you got me, so what?"

Jeffrey picked up his flashlight. "We think Keller might have something to do with the murder we were framed for."

Brian laughed. "Now you're really stretching."

"Tell us what you know," Jeffrey said.

Brian hesitated.

"Tell us," Jeffrey said, "or this time I won't hold Pablo back." He paused a moment and added, "Or myself."

Brian eyed the two boys in front of him. He knew exactly what Brian was thinking. In the small confines of the closet, it would be two against one. Jeffrey's frame was still large, but it was solid now, and he had grown an inch taller since Brian last saw him. He seemed almost brutish. Pablo was also taller and he was more muscular than ever. But it was Jeffrey's voice, a low, threatening tone that Brian had not heard from Jeffrey before that decided him. He sat down on a cardboard box and said, "Yeah. Yeah, it was Keller."

"How did it start?"

"Man, this was back before Christmas. I was halfway home from school one day when I realized I forgot my jacket. It was a Friday and I didn't want to be without it all weekend so I went back. The doors at the front entrance were locked so I went around to the gym and found a door that was open. I passed the locker room and something smelled funny so I stuck my head inside and there was Keller, sitting on a bench, getting high."

"Getting high on what?"

"Weed. He almost fell on the floor when he saw me. I told him I wouldn't tell anyone, but just to be sure I wouldn't talk, he gave me a little of his stuff. So I returned the favor. I stole a bottle of booze from my dad's liquor cabinet and gave it to him the next day. From then on he started sharing his stuff with me."

"You were smoking it?"

"Yeah, man. Every day. That's when my grades went down. My dad had a fit. He knew I was the one stealing his booze and now I was flunking all my classes. He told me if I flunked one more class he was going to send me to a military academy and he meant it." He looked up at the two boys. "So you see I was desperate. I had to pass Beasley's history class."

"So you broke into school," Jeffrey said, "and stole the answers to that test we had on the American Revolution."

"Yeah," Brian said. "I hid in the kitchen for a couple of hours after school. Those ashes you found on the kitchen floor were from me smoking a cigarette and waiting. When I was sure everyone was gone I climbed up through the ceiling panels and then through the vent and into the teacher's lounge. Beasley's locker was open so it was easy to find the test. They have a copy machine up there so I copied the answers, put the original back, and climbed back down to the kitchen. Keller didn't set the alarm, so all I had to do was set it myself and slip out the gym door."

"You walked from the kitchen to the gym?"

Brian shook his head. "I crawled low and went out that side door in the kitchen that leads to the gym, then crawled behind the bleachers to the gym door. That way I was only on camera for a second when I set the alarm and went out the door. Now I don't even worry about the cameras. Nobody even checks them unless the alarm goes off."

"What about the back door to the kitchen getting kicked in and all that?"

"That was Keller's idea. He was high when we came up with the whole plan and he thought somebody might catch on to me hiding in the kitchen, so I came back at four in the morning and faked the whole thing. I wore this same hoodie I'm wearing now so no one could see my face. Easy as ice cream pie."

"How'd you kick in the back door?" Pablo asked.

"Keller left it unlocked and unlatched." He looked at Jeffrey. "You were right all along, Jones. It was an inside job."

"So you did cheat on the test," Pablo said, "but you tried to pin it on Jeffrey and get him suspended."

Brian shrugged.

"And tonight the same routine?" Jeffrey said.

"Nah, man. That was just the first time. Since then I've been using the alarm code to sneak in."

"The alarm code that Keller gave you?"

Brian nodded. "That's how I got in here tonight. What about you guys? The doors are all locked. How'd you get in?"

"Don't worry about it," Pablo said.

"You think I'm stupid? Somebody helped you sneak in here and it wasn't Keller."

"Nobody helped us."

"Liar. I know somebody helped you. Don't worry, I'll figure it out."

"Tell us more about Keller," Jeffrey said.

"I already told you everything. But I don't see what Keller has to do with your murder trial. If that's what you think, why don't you snoop around in his office?"

Jeffrey's eyebrows arched high. "Keller has an office?"

"Yeah. It's a stock room really, but he calls it his office. You didn't know that? It's down the hall from the cafeteria. I'll show you." He stood up, went to the door, and pulled his hood over his head. "You're not worried about the cameras?"

"We're already wanted," Pablo said.

"Good point."

Brian opened the door and stepped out. Jeffrey and Pablo followed him. The three of them strode down the hallway, Brian a step ahead of the others.

"I roam the halls here at night," Brian said. He rapped a locker with his fist as he passed it. The clang of reverberating metal echoed down the hallway. "Cindy Baker's locker. Know what's in it? Her diary. I read every word. She's a nut case." Brian rapped another locker. "Norma Sandstrum. I read her diary too. She likes you, Reyes."

"Really?" Pablo said.

Brian rapped another locker. "Amy Burrell. She likes Jose Cruz in our history class. She has his pictures inside her math book."

"How are you getting into all these lockers?"

"Keller showed me. There's a master combination that opens every locker in the school." Brian rapped another locker. "Susie Norris." He turned and smirked over his shoulder. "Jones, you should see what she writes about you in her diary."

Jeffrey's face flamed red in the dark of the hallway. Brian cackled.

"Do all of these girls have diaries?" Pablo asked.

"Not all. But you'd be surprised how many do. Some of them leave their phones in their lockers overnight, because they don't want their parents reading their texts or seeing their search results. But I see them. I know every bit of gossip that goes on in this school. I rule this place." He banged a locker for emphasis. They turned a corner in the hall and Brian said, "There's one girl that really likes you, Reyes, but you already know who it is."

"Who?"

"Her initials are M.R."

Jeffrey stiffened. He was happy for Pablo, but inside he felt lonely and hollow. Brian sensed his discomfort and said, "What's the matter with you, Jones?"

Jeffrey ignored the question and said, "If you're smart enough to sneak into school without getting caught, then you're smart enough to pass Beasley's tests without cheating."

"I don't see it that way. I wish I did, but I don't." He suddenly laughed.

"What's so funny?" said Pablo.

"I was just thinking, you two guys were always the best. The best student, the best athlete, you did everything right. Me? I did everything wrong. But look what happened. You guys are the ones in trouble with the cops and I'm free as a bird. Funny how life works, isn't it?"

"Yeah," Pablo said, "a real laugh riot."

"This is it," Brian said and they stopped before a door at the end of the hallway. Jeffrey tried the knob, but the door was locked.

"I got it," Brian said. He pulled a knife from his pocket, opened the blade and slid it into the crevice in the door frame. A couple of jolts with the knife and the door jimmied open. Brian reached his hand inside the room and turned on the light.

The three boys stepped inside. Ahead of them was a narrow corridor with a desk, a filing cabinet, and cardboard boxes stacked to the ceiling with cleaning products and toilet paper.

"Have at it," Brian said.

Jeffrey turned to Pablo. "Take the desk. I'll take the filing cabinet. Look for anything unusual, any type of clue. Just be careful to arrange everything back the way it was."

"Got it," Pablo said.

Brian watched as the boys went to work. He grinned. "We're partners in crime now."

"Not hardly," Pablo said. He went through the top drawer of the desk and found a wholesale catalog for ordering cleaning products, two candy bars, and a coffee mug. He reached for the middle drawer and pulled it open. On top were two of Keller's work shirts. Pablo pulled the shirts out and set them gingerly on the desk, being careful to keep them folded just as he found them. Underneath the shirts was an empty binder, and under the binder was a clear plastic ten ounce bag of marijuana. Pablo stared at the bag. Brian saw it and his eyes widened. "Whoa, give me that." He reached for the bag.

Pablo pushed Brian's hand away. "Get out of here."

"Come on, let me have it."

"If you take it, he'll know someone's been in here."

"Give me just a little then."

"No, man, I mean it."

Jeffrey turned from the file cabinet. "What is it?"

Brian answered, "Keller's stash."

"It's drugs," Pablo said. "A bag of weed."

Jeffrey frowned. "Leave it, Brian. We can't let anyone know we've been in here."

Brian stepped back and shook his head. "I knew it was a mistake bringing you guys here."

"What do you want that stuff for anyway?" Pablo said. "It'll ruin your life."

Brian's voice was low and quiet. "My life's already ruined."

"Seriously, man," Pablo said. "Drugs will kill you."

"Spare me the lecture, Reyes. You got your little detective club. You got your friends. Me, I don't have anything. I don't belong to no club and I don't have any friends."

Jeffrey looked at him with surprise. Brian had always been so tough, but now he was slouched against the wall, all the cockiness and arrogance drained from his face.

"Keep looking," Jeffrey said, and turned back to the file cabinet. Each drawer of the cabinet was stuffed to capacity with files and each file was half an inch thick. Jeffrey had to pull six inches of files out of each drawer and set them on top of the cabinet just to have enough room to flip through the remaining ones. Most of the papers inside the files were safety and inspection reports, some dating back decades.

The first two drawers of the cabinet yielded nothing of note. The third drawer was stuffed like the others. Jeffrey pulled out a dozen file folders and set them on top of the cabinet. He began flipping through the remaining files in the drawer. The third file he flipped open stopped him cold. Inside, was a framed picture of Zinka. For a moment, he merely stared at the picture. Then he pulled the file out of the drawer and looked closer at the picture. The girl in the photo had brown hair, but it was definitely Zinka.

"Pablo," he said quietly, "Come look at this."

Pablo and Brian crowded in close behind him and looked at the picture.

"That's her," Pablo said.

"You guys know her?" Brian said.

"Do you?"

"I met her once. Keller told me she was his girlfriend."

Pablo turned to him with a look of shock on his face. "Are you serious? Where did you meet her?"

"In the parking lot outside."

"That's it," Pablo shouted. "That's our whole case."

Brian looked confused. "What's your whole case?"

Pablo pointed to the picture. "This is the girl that set us up. But nobody believes she exists. With this picture and with you as a witness, we can prove she's real."

"Whoa, wait a second. Fifteen minutes ago you guys wanted to kick my ass. Now you want me to be a witness?"

"We *need* you to be a witness."

"Yeah, right. You guys get out of jail and I go in."

Pablo spoke fast. "You don't have to say anything about breaking into school. We just need you to testify that you met this girl in the school parking lot and that Keller told you she was his girlfriend. Right, Jeffrey? What did she say her name was when you met her?"

"Zinka."

"That's it!"

Jeffrey said, "When did you see her, Brian?"

"Two weeks ago."

"Then she'll be on the parking lot cameras," Pablo said.

Jeffrey's face was serious. "Brian, will you testify?"

"Testify to who?"

"To the police and in court."

"No way."

"You have to," Pablo said.

"I don't have to do anything, Reyes."

"Brian, listen to me," Jeffrey said. "Our lives are at stake. We need you to tell the police everything you just told us, and we need you to testify to it under oath in a court of law."

"And you actually think that's going to get you out of jail?"

"It's a start. There are some other parts to this case we still have to unravel, but at least this will prove that Zinka exists, and that she visited our school."

"And what are you going to tell the police when they ask you where you got that picture?"

"I don't know, we'll make something up. Or maybe we'll just tell them the truth. But we'll leave your name out of it. We'll say we ran into you on the street, or contacted you at your house, or something. We'll fix our stories later, before we go to the police. Right now, we just need you to agree to testify."

Brian shrugged.

"Come on, man," Pablo said. "We need your help."

Brian shrugged again and said, "All right."

"Yes!" Pablo said.

Brian added hastily, "But you better come up with a good story, because I'm not going to jail over this."

"We will," Pablo assured him. "We're good at coming up with stories."

"And you guys are going to owe me big time."

"We know," Pablo said. "Thank you." He gave Brian a pat on the back.

Brian pulled a pack of cigarettes from his pocket, pulled a cigarette from the pack, and casually put it between his lips. "Anytime, man, anytime."

"Let's get out of here," Jeffrey said. "Put everything back the way you found it, except for this picture." He indicated the photo of Zinka. "It's coming with me."

Chapter Fourteen

"He what?"

Mr. Beasley's hair was sticking out in wild tufts. Jeffrey sat next to him in the passenger seat of the teacher's car. Pablo sat in the back seat. Outside, the night was still black.

"He said he would figure it out," Jeffrey said.

"Figure out who helped you sneak into school?"

"That's what he *said*, but that doesn't mean he will."

Mr. Beasley peered out the car windows. "He could have followed you here."

Pablo said, "Nah, we ditched him. We made sure of that."

"Did he see you set the alarm?"

Pablo shook his head. "We let him do it so he wouldn't know we had the alarm code. I don't think you have to worry, Mr. Beasley. Brian is dumb as a rock."

"He might be dumb as a rock when it comes to school work, but with anything sneaky, underhanded or suspicious his IQ rises to genius level. Believe me, he'll figure out I'm the one who helped you. And if he tells anyone, I'm ruined. I'll be joining you in the cell block."

"He can't do that," Jeffrey said. "If he does, he'll go to jail too."

"He could hold it over my head. Blackmail, you see?"

"But then you could do the same to him. So there's a deterrent on both sides."

"It's like the Cold War," Pablo said. "You taught us about that in class, remember, between Russia and the United States? Neither side can attack the other or they both get blown up."

Mr. Beasley grunted.

Jeffrey said to him, "I think the worst is over as far as you're concerned."

"How can you say that when I'm harboring two fugitives? Sneaky little cheater, eh? Just wait till I grade his next test."

Jeffrey frowned. "Actually, Mr. Beasley, you might want to give him an A. Just in case."

The teacher scoffed.

"Here's the good news," Jeffrey said, and he showed Mr. Beasley the picture of Zinka. "This is the girl who paid me and Pablo to find the guy who was killed. At the trial, they said she didn't exist."

Mr. Beasley studied the photo. "So this is the mystery woman, eh?"

"We found it in Keller's office. Brian told us he met her in the school parking lot, and that Keller said she's his girlfriend."

Mr. Beasley raised an eyebrow.

"We also have this." Jeffrey pulled Keller's file out from under his shirt. "It has Keller's job application, his medical history, and some other stuff." He looked at Mr. Beasley. "I need to use your computer right away to check some of this information."

The teacher shook his head. "Tonight is too risky, Mildred might wake up. Besides," he checked his watch, "it's almost two o'clock in the morning. And tomorrow's Sunday, Mildred will be home all day. Stay in my car in the garage all day tomorrow. I'll sneak you some food when she takes her bath. You can do your investigating Monday morning after she leaves for work. I'll call the school and tell them I'm sick and won't be in. Between the three of us, we should be able to get to the bottom of this whole mystery."

He started the car and pulled away from the curb. A hundred yards behind, a black sedan sat parked under a clump of trees. Inside the car, a match sizzled as it ignited and illuminated the grim face of Bill Keller. He used the match to light a cigarette and watched as Mr. Beasley's car drove to the first intersection and turned. Keller shook the match, threw it out the open window, and started his car.

An hour later, Mr. Beasley's car was safely parked in the teacher's garage. Jeffrey lay sprawled in the dark across the front seat, unable to sleep. His mind raced with the events of the past two hours. They were halfway to freedom. If they could just piece together a few remaining pieces, he and Pablo could prove their innocence. From the backseat he heard a whispered voice, "Jeffrey, you awake?"

"Yeah," Jeffrey whispered back. "I thought you were sleeping."

"I can't, my knee hurts too much. Every time I feel like I'm about to doze off, the pain shoots through it and wakes me up."

"We should have asked Beasley for an ice pack. I can sneak into the kitchen and get some ice."

"No, don't do that." The car was silent. Minutes passed. Pablo said, "I know it's impossible, but I wish we could see our parents and my sister Maria. If our plan fails and we go back to jail, they'll throw us in solitary confinement, and then we'll never see them again."

"I thought about that," Jeffrey said quietly.

Pablo's voice held a deep longing. "Do you think there's a way we could sneak up, just to see them one last time? They don't have to see us. I just want to see them. I want to remember what they look like."

Jeffrey said cautiously, "I don't think we can risk it. They probably have both of our houses under surveillance. They'd catch us fast."

There was a long pause. Jeffrey thought he heard a sniffle. Pablo said, "I understand."

Jeffrey stared into the darkness around him. He had the same sense of desperation as Pablo and he felt a panic rising in his body. To quell his fear he thought of Marisol. In his mind, he saw her: the black bangs that covered her forehead, the sparkle in her brown eyes. She was smiling now and the image calmed him. He took long, slow breaths. He suddenly felt very tired and he slid into the shaky realm between sleep and consciousness. Marisol was still in front of him, in his dream, but she seemed far off, like someone he had known in the distant past. The thought of losing her frightened him more than anything. Each time he reached for her, she drifted further and further away. In desperation he tried to run toward her, but his feet wouldn't move. Her image began to fade and dissolve. In seconds it was gone. Jeffrey woke up with a start, sweating and panting for air.

Chapter Fifteen

The high school hallway was silent save for the clacking of Marisol's shoes on the tile floor. The sound echoed against the walls and down the long hall, alerting the hall monitor at the far end, the same lanky boy that Jeffrey and Pablo had passed weeks ago.

Marisol was on her way to the principal's office. Now she knew how the two boys must have felt when Mr. Beasley marched them down the hall to Mr. Popper's office. The difference was they had each other. She was alone.

Marisol showed the boy her pass. He smirked and waved her on. As Marisol stepped past him, the boy looked her up and down and whispered in a taunting voice, "Busted." Marisol fought the urge to turn around and give him an earful. She kept walking.

The door to Mr. Popper's office was open. Marisol stopped in the open doorway and peered inside. Mr. Popper was behind his desk, talking to another man seated in front of him. The man in front of Mr. Popper was dressed in a suit. All Marisol saw of him was the back of his bald head. She waited. Mr. Popper spotted her and stood up. "Come in, Marisol, come in. Close the door behind you."

The bald man rose out of his chair to face her. Stitches covered his forehead and top of his skull. He was Peter Wingate, the policeman whose car had been stuck on the railroad tracks.

"Marisol Rodriguez?" he said.

Marisol nodded.

"I'm Officer Wingate, Los Angeles Police Department." He flashed a badge.

Mr. Popper pointed to an empty chair. "Please, sit down. Officer Wingate would like to ask you a few questions."

Marisol felt her heart beating rapidly. Wingate came to the point immediately. "I'm here to talk about your two friends, Jeffrey Jones and Pablo Reyes."

Marisol stiffened. She could feel her facial muscles moving involuntarily and she struggled to hold them still, to show no emotion at all.

"I know you're in contact with them," Wingate said, and he watched for her reaction.

Marisol stared back at him, her lips tightening. Her heart was pounding so loud, she thought the policeman could surely hear it. Did he really know she had talked on the phone with Jeffrey and Pablo? There was no way he could possibly know that. The policeman waited; waited for her to either confirm or deny. A full minute passed. Marisol said nothing.

Wingate said, "I think your friends are innocent. They saved my life, and they saved the life of a man in a restaurant on Saturday. Those aren't the actions of killers."

He paused again, waiting for Marisol to speak. She said nothing. Wingate said, "I want to help your friends, but to do that, I have to speak to them."

Marisol felt the eyes of both men on her.

Mr. Popper said. "Marisol, I want to help the boys too. I've maintained their innocence from the beginning, you know that. But I'm not going to ask you to lie to protect them. Just listen to what this officer is saying."

Wingate said, "They were involved in a dangerous chase the other day. Thank God nobody was injured or killed, but next time they could be." He reached in his pocket for a business card and handed it to her. "Just so you know, this is off the record. I want you to tell your friends that I came to see you and I want to help them. Tell them to call me at the phone number on that card. Understand?"

Marisol looked down at the business card in her hand.

"Understand?"

Marisol said nothing.

There was a sharp rap on the door. The door opened and Mrs. Stockton, the school nurse, leaned into the room, her face drawn and pale, and her voice breathless. "I'm sorry to interrupt, Mr. Popper. It's an emergency. There was a fight between Mr. Keller and a student. The student is injured."

Mr. Popper raised his eyebrows. "What student?"

Mrs. Stockton glanced nervously at Marisol and Wingate, and said, "Brian McHugh."

"Take a look," Jeffrey said, "it's all there."

Mr. Beasley looked up from his seat on the sofa in his living room and Jeffrey handed him Keller's file. He had spent the last three hours doing research on Mr. Beasley's computer in his home office. Mildred Beasley had left earlier that morning for her own teaching job. Pablo sat on the sofa next to Mr. Beasley and scooted in close to look. Jeffrey pulled up a chair across from them. Mr. Beasley flipped the file open. On top was Keller's job application.

"Keller was hired to work at our school last October," Jeffrey said, "but look where he worked before that."

Mr. Beasley looked at the job application. "Custodian, Saint Anthony's High School, New York from March until August of last year."

"Right," Jeffrey said. "I checked the crime statistics in New York for those six months; murders, assaults, everything. One crime stood out: an unsolved jewelry heist in Manhattan last July. A well-dressed girl walked in and asked to see a diamond necklace. While the clerk was distracted and opening the case to show her, two armed men wearing masks came in and robbed the place. They disabled the cameras and then they all left, the two men and the girl, with twelve million dollars in stolen jewels."

Mr. Beasley looked up with questioning eyes. "That's it? That's all you have?"

"Wait, there's more. Look at where Keller worked before he was in New York."

Mr. Beasley frowned down at Keller's job application. "Middleton High School, London. He was there six months also."

Pablo said, "Hodges is from London."

"Exactly," Jeffrey said, "and what happened in London while Keller was there? Another unsolved jewelry store robbery, the same way as the one in New York. A girl walks in, asks to see a diamond necklace and then two masked men come in and rob the place. This time they didn't disable the surveillance cameras and they got a good shot of the girl. I printed it. Here she is."

Jeffrey reached in his shirt pocket and pulled out a paper folded in fourths. He unfolded the paper and handed it to Mr. Beasley. The teacher looked down at a picture of a well-dressed blond girl, who looked to be in her late teens, standing at the counter of a jewelry shop. Pablo saw the picture and sat up excitedly. "It's Zinka!"

Mr. Beasley raised an eyebrow. "The mystery girl?"

"Yes, that's her," Pablo said.

"Where's that picture of her you took from the school?"

Jeffrey ran out of the room, retrieved the picture from Mr. Beasley's office, and came back. He handed the picture to Mr. Beasley and the teacher compared them. Jeffrey stood and watched.

"That's her with blond hair," Pablo said, pointing at the image captured by the surveillance cameras. "She had blond hair like that when we met her." He pointed to other picture. "That's her with brown hair."

Mr. Beasley nodded. "There is a startling resemblance."

"It's her," Pablo said emphatically.

Mr. Beasley looked up at Jeffrey, standing before him. "So what's your theory? How does this all tie together?"

"They're a pack of jewel thieves," Jeffrey said. "Keller, Zinka and Hodges, and they've been working together at least since last year in London."

"Then why is Keller a janitor?"

"That's a front, while they set up their robberies. My theory is the three of them robbed that jewelry store in New York and then Hodges double-crossed the other two and came out here with the stolen jewels. That's why he was tortured and his house was searched. Keller and Zinka were after the stolen jewels, but they couldn't find them."

"You suspect the killers were Keller and this girl?"

"Who else?"

Pablo said, "It also means they didn't find the jewels when they killed him. If they had, they would have took off, but Keller is still working at the school, holding his cover job."

"How do you know the dead man didn't sell the stolen jewels?" Mr. Beasley asked.

"Two reasons," Jeffrey said. "First, he would've hidden the money somewhere at his house and his killers would have found it. Second, I did a background search on Hodges. He actually had a job with the Santa Monica Parks and Recreation Department. A cover job like Keller's. If he had sold the jewels, he wouldn't be working. He'd have taken the money and either hid it or skipped town."

Pablo's face flushed with excitement. "That means all we have to do is find the stolen jewels and we should have enough evidence to clear our names."

"Right!"

"Hold on a second." Mr. Beasley rose to his feet. "You're saying that Keller, along with the fellow who was killed and this girl named Zinka comprised a trio of jewel thieves, and the dead fellow double-crossed Keller and the girl and absconded with the stolen jewels? Then he was killed and the two of you framed for his murder?"

Jeffrey nodded.

"Meanwhile," Mr. Beasley said, "the stolen jewels are still at large?"

Jeffrey nodded again. "That sums it up perfectly. My best guess is they were setting Brian up to frame him for the murder, only they couldn't find Hodges. Then we came along and everything fell into place. It was the perfect crime, except Hodges didn't talk and they never recovered the jewels. If they had, Keller wouldn't still be working at the school. He and Zinka would have disappeared weeks ago."

Mr. Beasley said, "So it's a double-cross times two. This Hodges fellow double-crossed Keller and the girl, and then Keller and the girl double-crossed both of you."

Pablo nodded. "A double double-cross."

"Right now it's just a theory," Jeffrey said. "But if we can find those stolen jewels, together with Brian's testimony about Zinka and these pictures we have of her, we should have enough evidence to go to the police. At least enough to show they're the ones behind the jewelry store robberies. Then if we can get the police to reopen the murder investigation, they should be able to figure out that Keller and Zinka are the ones who killed Hodges. But first we have to find those stolen jewels."

Pablo said excitedly, "It's a treasure hunt, Mr. Beasley."

"Indeed, it is. But where do you hide a fortune in stolen jewels. It could be anywhere. Buried, submerged ..."

"Or hidden in plain sight," Pablo said.

"Listen, if you're right about those stolen jewels, I'll go to the police with you. But how the blazes do you expect to find them without a single clue?"

"Actually, we have a couple of clues," Jeffrey said. "Hodges is from London, so there could be a London connection to where the jewels are hidden. He's also a chess player, so there could be a connection there. That's two clues. We know Hodges didn't have the jewels where he lived, because his killers searched the place. Unless ... unless there's a hidden panel or some kind of secret hiding place." He turned to Pablo. "We might have to sneak in there and look."

Mr. Beasley shook his head. "No, no, no, no, no. With the two of you on the run, it's simply too dangerous. Plus, after your incident in the restaurant, they know what both of you look like now." He nodded at Jeffrey. "That bald head of yours is like a giant neon sign flashing the words ARREST ME."

Jeffrey frowned down at the floor. "You might be right."

"Of course, I'm right."

A thought occurred to Jeffrey and he looked up, eyes gleaming. "You could do it, Mr. Beasley."

"Do what?"

"Sneak into Hodges' house and search for a secret panel."

"Me? Absolutely not."

"But the jewels might be there."

"Remember what you told us?" Pablo said. "You said when one is on a treasure hunt all propriety goes out the window."

Mr. Beasley pushed himself off the sofa. "I told you once already: don't repeat to me what I said in the past.

"But you said it."

"I know I said it, but if you think for one second that I'm going to sneak into a home where a murder occurred to search for a secret panel concealing stolen jewels, you're both lunatics."

The boys sat glumly.

Jeffrey said, "Well maybe the jewels are hidden someplace else."

Pablo turned to him. "You said Hodges worked for the Parks and Recreation Department in Santa Monica."

"Right."

"So maybe he hid the jewels close to where he worked."

Mr. Beasley raised an eyebrow, and Jeffrey said, "Go on."

"He was also a chess player. Remember when we talked about chess clubs? There's a chess club in Santa Monica at one of the parks with giant chess pieces and a giant board."

Mr. Beasley stepped closer. "I know that park, I've been there."

"So maybe Hodges hid the jewels someplace at that park."

"Pablo, it's brilliant," Jeffrey said. He turned to Mr. Beasley. "We have to go there immediately."

"To uncover a fortune in stolen jewels?"

"Yes, and to clear our names."

The boys waited. The teacher did not speak.

Pablo said, "Please, Mr. Beasley."

Mr. Beasley sat down and rubbed his chin. "I suggest we wait until evening, after the park is closed. Right now there are people milling all about. We may have to sneak in, but we'll do it under cover of night."

Pablo said, "If we get caught sneaking in, we'll all get arrested, including you."

Mr. Beasley nodded. "I am aware of the risk, but you're forgetting one thing."

"What's that?"

The teacher grinned. "When one is on a treasure hunt, all propriety goes out the window."

Chapter Sixteen

Night had settled in Santa Monica when Mr. Beasley pulled his car to the curb and he, Jeffrey and Pablo exited the vehicle. Homeless tents were pitched along the sidewalk, dozens of them, and from the occasional tent came the sound of rhythm and blues music playing on a radio. The only other sound came from the ocean as it lapped against the rocky shore and washed up onto the beach.

Mr. Beasley removed a black bag from the trunk of his car and he and the two boys walked briskly past the sidewalk tents to the chess park. Pablo, limping, tried his best to keep up with the other two. Jeffrey offered a hand, but Pablo waved him off.

A dozen scraggly homeless men were congregated around the palm trees near the park and from them the smell of cigarette tobacco drifted strongly downwind. They watched curiously as Jeffrey, Pablo and Mr. Beasley climbed over the low wall that surrounded the park.

Inside the small park were wooden benches and tables with chess boards embedded on the tables. The tables surrounded a giant chess board implanted onto the ground.

Jeffrey spoke quietly. "Let's start with the benches."

They split up and worked their way around the small park, running their hands over the tops and bottoms of the tables and benches and examining every inch. Finding nothing unusual, they moved to the giant chess board on the ground.

"Listen for a hollow sound," Jeffrey said, and he bent down low and tapped with his knuckles across a square on the chess board. Pablo and Mr. Beasley did the same. Fifteen minutes later they had covered the entire chess board and found nothing. The giant chess pieces were locked behind a wire cage and they stepped closer to it.

Mr. Beasley opened the black bag and extracted a pair of bolt cutters. "I'm only doing this in the name of justice," he said.

"We know that," Pablo told him. He and Jeffrey moved in close to shield the teacher from view. Mr. Beasley made the sign of the cross and used the bolt cutters to snap the padlock on the wire cage. He swung the gate open and pulled out the first piece, a black pawn that reached up to his knees.

Jeffrey held his ear close to the oversized pawn and tapped up and down the length of it with his knuckles. He tipped it onto its side and inspected the bottom. "It's solid," he said.

Mr. Beasley pulled out two more pawns. Jeffrey and Pablo inspected them both and shook their heads. After a dozen pieces they were sweating and breathing heavily. Pablo said, "I have an idea." The others turned to him. "Hodges was English and the English national anthem is *God Save the Queen*. Why don't we try the queen pieces next?"

Jeffrey and Mr. Beasley exchanged a look and the teacher reached for the large white queen piece. He rolled it out of the cage. Jeffrey put his ear close to listen and tapped up and down both sides, then he rolled the piece onto its side. His hand felt along the bottom of the piece and his fingers detected a small latch. "There's something here," he said.

Pablo and Mr. Beasley leaned in close. Jeffrey scraped his fingers against the latch and pulled. A small panel came off. He leaned down close to look and his eyes widened. "I think we found it," he said excitedly. He reached inside the bottom of the chess piece and pulled out a sparkling diamond necklace.

Mr. Beasley saw the necklace and exclaimed, "We've done it."

"There's more," Jeffrey said. He pulled another diamond necklace out of the chess piece, followed by another. "Mr. Beasley, give me that bag," he said, and to Pablo, "Keep an eye out. Make sure no one can see us."

The homeless men were no longer watching, but Pablo positioned himself to block Jeffrey from their view anyway. Jeffrey scooped the diamond necklaces into the bag, along with more jewels he pulled from the hollowed out bottom of the chess piece. "Pablo, you're a genius," he said.

On the drive back, Pablo counted the haul.

"Twenty-six diamond necklaces. At least, I think they're diamonds. I'm no expert, but I don't know what else they could be. Thirteen diamond rings. Some stars that look like they're covered in diamonds. Some things with pins on them that are covered in gold and diamonds. This stuff must be worth a fortune." He stared at the jewels before him and in a somber tone he said, "How do we turn this stuff in?"

"I was thinking tomorrow morning," Jeffrey said, "but to be fair, we should take a vote. What do you say, Mr. Beasley?"

The teacher laughed. "You want me to vote?"

"It's only fair," Jeffrey said. "You're mixed up in this now too."

Mr. Beasley said, "Even with those jewels there's no guarantee the police will believe you or that you'll get your convictions overturned. In fact, the first thing they'll do is arrest you and they won't be very friendly about it either."

"I know," Jeffrey said, "but at this point there's not much more we can do."

"Then I say the sooner the better and tomorrow morning is probably the best time."

Jeffrey turned to the backseat.

Pablo nodded. "Tomorrow morning sounds good, but we should have our parents and the lawyers there. They can help us present all our evidence. We can even bring Brian so he can tell them about Zinka."

"I'll go with you, as well," said Mr. Beasley. "It goes without saying that I'm proud of both of you."

The boys thanked him. Jeffrey said, "Wait, I just thought about something, Mr. Beasley. They'll probably arrest you too, for helping us."

"We can leave you out," Pablo said. "We can say we did all this on our own and not mention your name."

Mr. Beasley shook his head. "One thing I've learned, honesty is the best policy. If it takes my getting arrested to help clear your names and set you free, so be it."

Pablo clapped Mr. Beasley on the back of his shoulder.

Jeffrey pulled his burner phone from his pocket. "I'll call Susie. I'll tell her to contact our parents and let them know everything that's happened."

He punched a number on the phone and lifted it to his ear. Susie answered and he said, "It's me."

Susie said, "Wait." A moment later, she was back on the line, her voice low and guarded. "Are you okay?"

He told her everything.

Susie said, "I knew you could do it, Jeffrey."

"Don't celebrate yet. We're still fugitives, and we'll have to go back to jail while the police sort it out."

Susie said, "Call Marisol. There's a policeman at her house right now. He says you saved his life and he wants to help you. Marisol hasn't told him anything, but he's talking to her mom."

Jeffrey thanked her and hung up. He told Pablo and Mr. Beasley about the policeman at Marisol's house. Pablo said, "It's probably that guy whose car we moved off the tracks."

They took another vote and decided to call. Marisol's mother answered the phone. Jeffrey said, "Mrs. Rodriguez, this is Jeffrey Jones."

He heard a loud gasp and some fumbling with the phone, and then a man's voice said, "This is Peter Wingate, Los Angeles Police Department."

Jeffrey told him about the jewels heists in London and New York, the hidden jewels they'd recovered, and all the information he had on Keller and Zinka. The policeman listened intently. He tried to talk Jeffrey into turning himself in immediately, but Jeffrey said he needed more time to compile his evidence and arrange for his parents and lawyer to attend. Wingate agreed to meet with them the following morning at the office of Jeffrey's lawyer. He gave Jeffrey his phone number. Jeffrey found a pen in the glove compartment of the car and wrote the number on the palm of his hand. "I believe you," Wingate said, "and I'll do everything I can to help you."

Jeffrey hung up and sat back with a smile.

Mr. Beasley turned the car onto his street and his eyes went to the driveway. "Mildred's car isn't here. She should have been home hours ago."

A figure moved by the front door and Pablo shouted, "There's someone at the door." He and Jeffrey ducked down out of sight.

Mr. Beasley drove closer to his house. "It's Brian McHugh."

Jeffrey and Pablo popped their heads up.

"What's he doing here?" Pablo said.

The teacher grunted. "I told you he'd figure out who was helping you. Well, nothing to fear now, we're all going to the police tomorrow. If he's going to testify on your behalf, we can bring him with us."

He turned the car into the driveway. Gravel popped loudly under the car's tires. Brian stepped down the walk toward them. His right cheek was bruised and swollen. Mr. Beasley and the boys climbed out of the car.

Brian nodded at the three of them and said, "I came to warn you guys."

"Warn us about what?" Pablo said.

"Keller's on to you. He pulled me aside in the hallway at school and wanted to know if I thought you might be hiding out here."

Jeffrey and Pablo froze. Pablo said, "What did you tell him?"

"I didn't tell him anything. I said it was a stupid idea; that you were probably on your way to Mexico. He didn't believe me and we got in a fight. He gave me this—" Brian pointed to his swollen cheek. "The police came, but he took off. He looked weird, man.

His eyes were all bloodshot, but he wasn't high. Anyway, I came to warn you."

"What did the police say?"

"Don't worry, I didn't talk. If I did, it would have given you guys away."

Jeffrey and Pablo thanked him.

Mr. Beasley's phone buzzed in his pocket. He checked the caller ID and answered.

The voice on the line was low and gruff. "Beasley?"

"Yes, speaking."

"We have your wife."

"Who is this?"

The boys saw the pale look on the teacher's face and watched.

The voice on the line said, "Shut up and listen. We have your wife. If you ever want to see her again, keep those two kids out of sight for the next twenty-four hours. If anyone goes to the police, either you or them, your wife is dead. Understand?"

Mr. Beasley stood perfectly still, not moving a muscle. "Yes," he said, "but listen to me—"

The voice cut him off. "No, you listen to me. Anyone goes to the police and she's dead. In twenty-four hours, we'll release her. That's the deal."

The line clicked off.

Mr. Beasley turned to the boys, his face drained of color. "They've kidnapped Mildred. They're threatening to kill her."

"Was it Keller?" Jeffrey asked.

"I don't know. It sounded like it could be him, but I'm not sure. He said they'll release her in twenty-four hours as long as we don't go to the police."

"He knew about us?"

"Yes."

"Then it's got to be Keller," Jeffrey said. "Don't you see? He's panicking. His whole crime is falling apart. That's why he attacked Brian. Brian's the only person who can connect him to Zinka. He's leaving the country tonight, maybe right now. Call him back."

"And say what?"

"Anything, we have to stall him. If he's taking a flight out of the country tonight, there's no way he could get your wife past all the security at the airport. He's probably going to kill her right now. Call him back - quick, Mr. Beasley."

Mr. Beasley fumbled with the phone and dialed.

The line picked up. There was a pause and the voice said, "Are you deaf? Did you not understand my instructions?"

"Yes, I understand, but—"

"We have the jewels!" Jeffrey shouted.

"Who's that?" the voice snapped.

Jeffrey motioned for Mr. Beasley to hand him the phone.

"Is that the smart kid?" the voice asked.

"Let me talk to him," Jeffrey whispered.

Mr. Beasley handed the phone to Jeffrey. Pablo and Brian crowded in close behind him.

Jeffrey tensed and raised the phone to his ear. "We have the jewels," he said.

"Who is this?" the voice said. It sounded like Keller, but Jeffrey wasn't sure. He replied, "This is Jeffrey."

"We have Beasley's wife, and we'll cut her throat if you don't do exactly what I say. Stay out of sight, stay hidden for the next twenty-four hours. After that we'll release her. Understand?"

"I understand, but how do we know she's still alive?"

Mr. Beasley's eyes opened wide.

There was a rustling sound on the line followed by a slap and a woman's scream. Jeffrey winced.

"Is that enough for you?" the voice asked.

"Yes, we won't go to the police. But there's something you should know. We have the jewels."

"What jewels?"

"The ones you want. The ones from the New York robbery."

There was a long pause. The voice said, "You're lying."

"Am I? Twenty-six diamond necklaces, thirteen diamond rings, a bunch of other stuff. We have it all." Jeffrey glanced at Mr. Beasley's blanched white face. "We'll make you a trade, the jewels for Mrs. Beasley."

There was another pause. The voice said, "Meet me at MacArthur Park in one hour. If you're not there, if the jewels aren't there, the woman is dead. If I see a cop car or anyone who even looks like a cop within a mile of that park, the woman's dead." The line clicked off.

Jeffrey lowered the phone. Mr. Beasley snatched it out of his hands and shouted, "The jewels for my wife? Are you insane?"

"What else could I do?" Jeffrey said. "I'm stalling for time and the jewels are the only thing we have to bargain with."

"What did he say?" Pablo asked.

"We have to be at MacArthur Park in one hour or no deal."

Pablo said, "Better start driving, Mr. Beasley. We can argue on the way."

The teacher cursed and hurried back to his car. The boys followed him, including Brian who said, "I'm coming too," and slid into the backseat with Pablo. The teacher turned the ignition and backed out of the driveway. "What if he kills her before we get there?"

Jeffrey said, "That's probably what he would have done if we hadn't called him. At least now we have a little time. We have time to think. We need a plan."

The car hit the street. Mr. Beasley put the car in drive and accelerated. "I think we should notify the police."

"He said if he sees a cop at the park, he'll kill her. I'll call Wingate." Jeffrey dialed the policeman's number and told him what happened.

"I'll meet you at the park," Wingate said, "but how do I recognize you? I didn't get a good look at you at the accident and I've never met your teacher."

"Bring Marisol," Jeffrey told him, "she knows us." He told Wingate of Keller's warning regarding the police.

"Don't worry," Wingate said, "I'm out of uniform."

Jeffrey hung up and filled Brian in on all the details. Pablo opened the black bag and showed Brian the stolen jewels.

Brian listened wide-eyed and attentive. He said, "I want to help you guys from now on. I want to be part of your club."

Pablo said, "Hurry, Mr. Beasley. Every second counts."

Chapter Seventeen

Mr. Beasley pulled his car over at the intersection of 6th Street and Lake Street and his phone rang immediately. The voice on the line spoke tersely, "Put the smart kid on the phone."

Mr. Beasley handed the phone to Jeffrey. The voice said, "You have the jewels?"

"We have the jewels," Jeffrey said.

"Leave the teacher."

"Why?" Jeffrey asked.

"Do it the way I'm telling you or the lady's dead."

"Hold on." Jeffrey covered the mouthpiece of the phone and spoke quietly to Mr. Beasley. "He wants you to stay here."

"I can't do that."

Jeffrey nodded up at the tall buildings on the opposite side of the street. "He might be watching us from one of those."

"I don't care, I have to go."

"He's threatening to kill Mrs. Beasley if you come."

Pablo whispered. "Just stay behind for a minute or two, and then follow us."

Mr. Beasley hit the steering wheel with his fist. He grimaced, turned to Jeffrey, and gave a short nod.

Jeffrey put the phone to his ear. "He'll stay behind."

"Do exactly what I say or the woman's dead. Go into the park, run down the path to your left and under the tunnel to the other side. You have one minute."

"Wait—"

The line clicked off.

"Come on," Jeffrey said. He bolted from the car with the teacher's phone in his hand. Pablo followed him, carrying the black bag and favoring one leg. Brian followed Pablo. Mr. Beasley opened his car door and climbed out. He watched the boys run off.

Homeless men lay sprawled on the grass around the sidewalk. The park behind them was closed and almost completely dark. The three boys ran past the homeless men and into the park. Jeffrey spotted a path to his left that sloped down a hill and then disappeared in the dark. Beyond that he could see nothing. He ran to it. Pablo followed, limping. Brian ran alongside of Pablo.

"Do you know where we're going?" Pablo asked.

"He said to follow this path to a tunnel," Jeffrey said, "but I don't see a tunnel."

Pablo pointed. "There it is."

Back at the street, a car pulled up behind Mr. Beasley. The teacher stiffened. The car doors popped open and Marisol and Wingate stepped out.

Marisol pointed. "That's Mr. Beasley."

Wingate stepped forward. "Where are the boys?"

"They ran that way." Mr. Beasley pointed. "The kidnappers told me to stay behind or they'd kill my wife."

Wingate pulled his service gun and ran into the park. Marisol and Mr. Beasley followed.

Jeffrey, Pablo and Brian ran into the pitch black tunnel. Three male figures stepped out of the shadows ahead of them. They were Hispanic teens, local gang members, a year older than the three boys and hard-looking, with sinewy muscles and tattoos. The tallest of the group carried a lead pipe. He stepped closer and said, "What are you doing in our park?"

"Just passing through," Pablo said.

"This is our park. You want to pass through our park, you gotta pay." He nodded at the bag in Pablo's right hand. "Give us the bag."

Jeffrey and Brian tensed.

Pablo said, "We can't do that."

There was a moment of hushed silence, and then the taller boy rushed forward and drew the pipe back. Pablo closed the gap and shot his fist into the boy's jaw. The boy staggered back. The other two boys rushed Jeffrey and Brian. Jeffrey grabbed his adversary and the two of them wrestled and stumbled to the ground. The third boy threw a punch at Brian and missed. Brian punched back and hit the boy in the jaw, dropping him. The boy with the pipe regained his footing and swung the pipe at Pablo's legs, hitting his injured knee. Pablo fell to the ground. Jeffrey swung his right arm under his opponent's right arm and clamped his hand against the back of the boy's neck, catching him in a half-nelson. He slammed the boy's head into the ground. Brian's opponent started to rise. Brian swung a kick at his stomach. The boy doubled over and vomited. The boy with the pipe charged Pablo and swung the pipe at his head. Pablo, still on the ground, covered his head and took the blow on his arms. The boy raised the pipe for another strike. Pablo swung his good leg and caught the boy on the back of his knee. The boy dropped and the pipe fell to the ground. The boy scrambled to his feet. Brian grabbed the pipe and faced him. The boy backed up several paces, turned, and ran away. Seconds later, his friends joined him and the three gang members ran from the tunnel.

Jeffrey, Pablo and Brian ran through the other end of the tunnel and emerged near the lake in the center of the park. Pablo hobbled behind the others. He ran several yards and collapsed on the walkway. Jeffrey and Brian ran to him. All three boys panted for breath.

Pablo's voice was quivering. "My knee, Jeffrey. I can't go on."

Jeffrey picked up the black bag. "Brian, give him a hand." The teacher's phone rang. Jeffrey answered quickly and the voice said, "Where are you?"

"We went through the tunnel like you said."

"Follow the lake to your right. Hurry." The voice waited.

Pablo put his arm around Brian's shoulders and the husky boy lifted Pablo to his feet and helped him walk. They followed Jeffrey around the massive lake.

"Where are you?" Jeffrey said into the phone.

"Keep walking."

The boys walked another twenty yards. The voice said, "Stop."

Jeffrey held the phone to his ear, while his eyes scanned the darkness. He saw movement in a clump of bushes atop a small hill ahead of him. Behind the hill was Wilshire Boulevard.

"Where are the jewels?" the voice on the phone said.

"I have them," Jeffrey said, and he lifted the bag.

"Show me."

"Show me Mrs. Beasley first."

Fifty yards behind them, Wingate, Marisol and Mr. Beasley ran into the darkened tunnel.

Jeffrey heard a car door open and close. He peered into the dark and saw movement in the thicket on the hill. Zinka stepped out from behind the bushes, followed by Mildred with a blindfold over her eyes. Zinka led Mildred by the arm slowly down the hill. As Zinka drew near, she forced a smile and said, "Hello, Jeffrey."

Pablo and Brian watched as Jeffrey handed her the bag. Zinka released Mildred, opened the bag, and looked inside. She smiled again and with a trace of sadness in her voice, she said, "I should have known you'd find them."

She forced another smile and started back up the hill, carrying the bag. A man stepped quickly out from behind the bushes with a gun in his hand. Jeffrey recognized the man at once. It was Keller. The hangdog look of the janitor was gone, replaced with the stone-cold face of a killer.

Jeffrey knew immediately what was going to happen. He grabbed Mildred by the arm and dove to the ground. Mildred screamed. Keller's gun cracked twice.

Jeffrey heard shouts and commotion behind him. Wingate leapt over him and scrambled up the hill. Then Mr. Beasley was at his side, covering Mildred's body with his own.

Shouts came from the hill above and more gunfire erupted. Jeffrey covered his head. His heart beat wildly against the rough concrete walkway. He heard a car door slam, tires squealing, and the sound of a car racing away on the street above.

Atop the hill, Wingate stood over Keller's lifeless body. The black bag lay on the ground next to Keller, its contents spilled out onto the grass. Wingate was on his phone, calling for help and reporting a car's license plate number. In Wingate's other hand was his revolver. Sirens wailed in the distance.

Jeffrey heard voices behind him and turned to see Brian sprawled on his back on the cold pavement, blood seeping from a bullet hole in his stomach. Pablo was kneeling at Brian's side. He held Brian's hand and pleaded, "Stay with me, Brian. Stay with me." Marisol clung fast to Pablo's shoulder and watched in horror.

Brian lay completely still, unable to move. His eyes held a glassy stare, his lips quivered as he tried to speak, but no sound came out.

Pablo pressed the boy's hand. "Stay with me," he said, his voice cracking. "Stay with me, Brian. Don't die, man. The ambulance is coming, just hold on. You're the toughest kid in our school. You can do it. You don't have to be alone anymore. You can join our club, you can be our friend. Just don't die. Come on, man. Come on!"

Brian's fingers turned cold and limp. Pablo squeezed his hand tighter. "Stay with me, man," he cried, tears streaming down his cheeks. "Stay with me. Just a little longer. You can do it, man. You're tough, you can do it! Stay with me, Brian! Stay with me!"

Pablo let out an anguished cry. Marisol burst into tears. Brian was dead.

Chapter Eighteen

It was raining again. Black clouds blanketed the sky and poured their tears down upon the city. Jeffrey could have taken a bus to the cemetery, but he chose to walk the four miles under an umbrella. He wanted time to think. He wanted to run the events of the last few months over and over in his mind. It had all happened so fast.

He replayed the image in his mind of Keller pulling his gun at MacArthur Park and opening fire. When the shooting started, Zinka hopped in her car and sped off. She was apprehended an hour later and confessed to the jewelry heists, the murder of William Hodges, and the framing of Jeffrey and Pablo. She also admitted that she and Keller had intended to murder Mrs. Beasley before making their getaway that night. It was only Jeffrey's quick thinking and the actions of the three boys that had saved Mildred Beasley's life.

Jeffrey and Pablo were arrested, held for a week while the police sorted everything out, and released. Jeffrey had been right all along, but it didn't change the fact that Brian was dead.

The cemetery was dark and deserted, except for a solitary figure, dressed in a black overcoat and standing alone under an umbrella at the side of the very grave Jeffrey himself had come to see. Jeffrey approached from behind, slightly unnerved. He had hoped he would be alone, and in this downpour, he thought he would be.

He crossed the expanse of lawn, his shoes sinking into the wet grass, the rain hammering a rhythm atop his umbrella. As he drew near he saw that the man standing beside Brian's grave was Father Pat.

Jeffrey stood next to him. For the first time in his life, he was taller than the old white-haired priest. Father Pat gave him a quick look and turned his eyes back to the grave. "Pablo wanted to come," Jeffrey said, "but he's still laid up, because of his knee. The doctors won't let him walk for a few more days."

Father Pat nodded.

"He's doing better," Jeffrey said.

Father Pat nodded again. There was a moment of silence, no sound save for the patter of the rain on their umbrellas. The old priest spoke quietly, *"Tell me,* said Saint Bernard, *where are the lovers of the world? Of them nothing remains save ashes and worms."* He paused. "The rich, the famous, the stars of yesterday, where are they now? Dead and rotting in the grave. The stars of today, where will they be tomorrow? Life is fragile, Jeffrey. So fragile and so brief. It passes in the blink of an eye and then we die. And where will our final resting place be? A few to heaven, many more to hell."

"Do you think Brian made it?" Jeffrey asked.

Father Pat nodded solemnly. "He came to me for confession the day before he was killed."

A look of surprise swept over Jeffrey's face.

"It was a long confession," Father Pat said quietly. "I absolved him. Now he's in his eternal resting place. He was fifteen. I'm ninety-two." The old priest's weathered face twisted suddenly and then the tears came, racking his body with convulsions.

Jeffrey put his arm around the older man's bony shoulders and pulled his body close to his own. He felt the frail man's body heave and press against his own with every sob. Then Jeffrey felt his own tears coming and he could not stop them. The rain pelted harder on their umbrellas.

Lightning crackled and lit up the cemetery like a giant flare, illuminating dozens of headstones and monuments. Then it was dark again and a low rumbling growl of thunder echoed across the sky.

The old man and the boy stood side by side in the rain and together they cried.

THANK YOU VERY MUCH for buying this book! If you enjoyed it, please share your thoughts by posting a review where you purchased the book. People often make their book-reading decisions based on other people's reviews (I know I do), and your review of this book could be the deciding factor for someone who is wondering whether or not to read it. Even a short, one sentence review will help. Thank you again.

Mike Mains writes mystery and adventure books for sleuths of all ages. He can be reached at mainsmike@yahoo.com

The North Hollywood Detective Club Series

THE CASE OF THE HOLLYWOOD ART HEIST

Jeffrey Jones is a kid with a problem. A *lot* of problems. He's laughed at in school. The neighborhood bully has it out for him. And his parents treat him like a six-year-old. However, Jeffrey does have one ace up his sleeve: He's a master investigator.

When the brother of a classmate is arrested for stealing a valuable painting, Jeffrey and his best friend, Pablo Reyes, form The North Hollywood Detective Club and set out to rescue him from jail. Their investigation leads them to a mysterious tattoo parlor, a glamorous television star, and a 20-year-old unsolved murder.

THE CASE OF THE DEAD MAN'S TREASURE

Hired by their teacher to find the driver responsible for a hit-and-run car accident, teen detectives Jeffrey Jones and Pablo Reyes stumble upon a search for an ancient treasure. Working feverishly to decipher the clues to the treasure's location, they find themselves in a race against time with a ruthless treasure hunter who will stop at nothing to get his hands on the prize.

THE CASE OF THE CHRISTMAS COUNTERFEITERS

Two teenage detectives. One criminal mastermind. And two billion dollars in counterfeit currency. What could possibly go wrong?

While the rest of the world prepares to celebrate Christmas, Jeffrey and Pablo stumble upon a plot to flood Los Angeles with billions of dollars in counterfeit money. Together with their friends Marisol and Susie, they uncover a master criminal, his hoodlum son, and a mysterious 15-year-old girl who holds the key to the entire puzzle.

Other Books by Mike Mains

MONKEY JOKES – A JOKE BOOK FOR KIDS!

Tickle your funny bone with these laugh-a-minute jokes for kids. Apes, cheetahs, gorillas, they're all here, ready to entertain you in the world's first and funniest collection of monkey jokes.

Are you ready for a gorillian laughs? Then stop monkeying around and get this book today!

BODYBUILDING FOR BOYS & YOUNG MEN

If you want muscles and you want them fast, this is the book for you. It's all here: what exercises to do, how often to exercise, what to eat, even how to think. A fast, fun and effective way to build your body. The bodybuilding program contained in this book has been tested hundreds of times and has a 100% success rate.

ANNIHILATE YOUR ACNE

Do you suffer from acne? I did – for many years – until I learned what causes acne and how to eliminate it. Once you eliminate the cause of acne, your skin clears up and your acne melts away like a snow cone on a warm summer day. It worked for me, it's worked for thousands of others, and it will probably work for you too. Learn how in this book.